VITA- NJA

the Garden of Shadows

SANDY ROBSON

VITA-MAN C and the MITT NINJA

the Garden of Shadows

SANDY ROBSON

Cover and Illustrations by
SANDY ROBSON

EDITED BY
TERESA MOONEY

For: Nicole, Cailum and Aidan.
You have given me and are my, everything.

THANK YOU TO:
Megan Hamilton
Mark Schoenberg
Paul Brown
Julie Weeks
Sherry and Kevin House
Carrie Ruscheinsky and Tyler Labine
David and Pam Dempsy
Deanna and Brian Nixon
Danielle and Michael Taylor
Barry Robson
Deena Mohammed
Lindsay and Chris Dawkins
Maureen and Mike Ruscheinsky
Lindsay Forslund
Kristen Kokotilo
Jaime Swiscoski
Trina Isobe
Sara Brown
Barb Ginn
Melanie Walden
Chris Woods
Ginny Taylor
Laureen Nowicki
John Kokotilo
Pamela Pike
Ainslie and Kornel Koopmans
Andrea Kokotilo
Michelle Reilly
Margaret Webb
Nancy Hodgkinson
Peter McAuley

For your support of this novel and your generous contribution to the
Hodgkinson/McAuley Bursaries
(Bursaries for graduating students with special needs and
learning disabilities to support the pursuit of their post
secondary dreams.)

"Never be afraid your shadow,

for it is in some of your darkest places,

that you will find your brightest light."

-SANDY ROBSON-

to ešt še

(the first scroll)

I whisper to my little brother, Aidan.

"Get in the corner and be quiet."

I can hear them coming. They're getting closer. I hear their feet dragging on the ground. They keep passing us, grunting and groaning, looking for more things to take. Sooner or later, they'll be coming for us! If I had one wish...it'd be that this day; the worst day of my entire life would just disappear. I've tried hard to stop it, but I'm only eleven and no one listens to an eleven year old. So, I'm doing the only thing I know how to do when I'm scared... I'm hiding.

My Dad and I built this fort when I was seven. It protected me from Gladis back then and it's been saving my butt ever since. Don't laugh, I know her name sounds like some old lady that pinches your cheeks, but her name is the only lady-like thing about her. That's why we call her Gladiator Gladis. She doesn't like horses, or frilly things and she especially hates butterflies. I once saw her snatch a butterfly out of the air with her teeth, then spit it out into her hand and then squish it between her fingers. She laughed the whole time; a deep, dark, crazy clown kind of laugh. She got her growth spurt, like five years early and she is so strong, I think she could even take my Dad. Gladis chased me home from school everyday that year. Mama said it's because Gladis likes me but Gladis says it's because she "doesn't like my stupid face." I think I'll take Gladis' side on this one. Running away from her isn't easy because with those freakishly long legs of hers, she's as fast as a cheetah. The only thing I could do to get away from her was to become an expert at diving over the hedges and climbing the fences between my school and home. But once I reached my block, that's where the fort came in. My Mama wasn't home until 3:45 on the dot, because back then, my little brother Aidan was in preschool and she had to pick him up everyday, which left me unprotected for forty-five whole minutes. So, when the bell rang, I'd run towards the gym and hang a tight left just before the gym doors and slip into Hector's office, the janitor. It wasn't really much of an office; just a bunch of water heaters and pipes, but it had a door that let out at the back of the school, and for a fruit roll-up, Hector would let me use it. From there I'd run through a bunch of backyards. After diving over five fences and twelve hedges, I would reach my block ahead of Gladis, but not by much. I'd give all the energy I had left and run to my house. When I got to it, I'd bypass my front door, because fumbling with keys takes too long, and shimmy down the skinny gap between our house and the garage. This is still the fastest shortcut to our backyard and a great place to jump out of and scare Mama when she comes home from grocery shopping. Gladis couldn't squeeze into the gap, so it gave me just the distance I needed. I'd to pop out the other side of the gap and into our backyard just a couple of feet from the rope ladder. Once I made it up to my tree fort, I'd yank the rope ladder up and Gladis or any other attacker was totally pwned. When Aidan got big enough to climb the rope ladder all by himself, I made him a member of the fort too. It was a simple ceremony; just he and I and a couple of tin foil hats. The only initiation I made him do was steal a giant pair of underpants off "Old Man Cummings'" clothesline. I'm sure you're wondering what a couple of kids wanted with a pair of old man's tighty-whities? Well, if you looked at our fort on a windy day you'd find the answer, flapping in the wind, high above our fort. Not only did they become our fort flag, but also they were the inspiration for our club colors; white, brown and yellow.

Even in the winter this place rocks. Dad put in electricity and in a few minutes, even on the coldest day, my little space heater has the fort toasty. Any time of year we can just kick back, grab a water or juice box from the little fridge and watch DVD's on an old TV, or laugh at epic fails on the internet, thanks to my Dad and the invention of WIFI. But, this fort isn't all fun and games; I also use it to get some serious work done. In the early spring, before the snow has melted, I plant my seeds up here. It's like magic, with row after row of colorful possibilities. It's so cool. You can turn a simple seed into the most amazing things. I make all my starter plants up here on my workbench because it's warm, quiet and most important, private, so none of the kids in the neighborhood can tease me.

The first thing I ever grew was a cherry tomato plant I call "Tommy". It's short for Tommy Toe. Every year I replant him, using the seeds from the first tomatoes it ever grew. Tommy is now 4 years old. So, actually this is Tommy's great-great-great-great grandson, but I still call him Tommy. One year I grew a huge Venus Fly Trap that really freaked Aidan out. He thought feeding it flies was murder, so he tried to make me feel bad by naming each fly I caught and forced me to have a funeral for each and every one of his "fly guys" every time I fed the plant. Thank goodness no one saw us, standing side-by-side, arms crossed and our heads down as Aidan hummed a sad tune. At the end of the song, he'd close his eyes and I'd tickle the little hairs on the inside of the plant's mouth with the fly and it would close around it. Aidan did a good job of making me feel guilty, because I actually started to feel bad for the flies. After a few funerals, I'd had enough and gave the Venus Fly Trap away to one of the kids on our block.

I turned 11 in September and for my birthday my parents gave me a "Jr. Inventors Kit". At first I thought it was pretty lame, but then Dad showed me how to make electricity using an orange peel, two wires and a light bulb. Since then, I've been making all sorts of inventions, like this telescope; one chip tube, a pair of old glasses and some tape and I can see things far away. I didn't know how important this invention would be when I made it, but now it's the most important thing I have. I rest my telescope on the edge of the window box that hangs off the front window of my fort and poke it through the flowers. I point it towards the front lawn and see Mama standing there, holding Dad's hula lamp. Since I built this telescope I've gotten pretty good at reading lips; that's how I found out that Suzie Parker thinks I'm gross. I'm reading Mama's lips as she calls for my Dad.

"Can I throw this out?" she asks and then her face all of a sudden looks sad.

I see her look down and I sweep my telescope down too, to see what's making her so sad. In front of Mama, her special flowers that line the front walk are all broken and stepped on. See, Mama has a "Green Thumb" too and her special flowers are unlike any flower anyone has ever seen before. The flowers are all bright colors and made up of the weirdest shapes. I can't find them in any book or on the Internet and we always have people driving by our house to take a look at them. People always ask her where she got them and she says they've been growing in her family's garden for generations.

I whip my telescope back up and catch my Dad running out of the house. He looks at the flowers and then his face gets red.

"I tell ya, these guys don't care about anything but the

time clock. They are like a stampede of bulls in a china shop."

Mama stops him.

"My mother gave me those flowers…we worked so hard to make them nice."

My Dad looks at her and takes her hand.

"I know. We did work hard."

I turn to Aidan.

"That's it, he's making his move. He's doing it!"

Aidan rushes over and tries to see out the window.

"Pashawn! Sashawn!" He says and I push him out of my way.

"I can read lips. I'll tell you everything that's happening, okay? Look, they're probably gonna kiss and that isn't something a little kid should see. But, that isn't gonna happen if you stop crossing, so I need you to use all your wishes and cross like you never crossed before!"

Aidan sits down on the floor and crosses his legs, he takes off his mittens and crosses his fingers and even crosses his eyes.

I look at him and then around our sacred fort, our hiding place. It's been were we go to escape the wrath of Gladis or get the best angle to launch an "Icer" from in a snowball fight. It's also the place we go when our parents need space to "Talk". Dad put lots of insulation in the walls, so it keeps us warm when we are cold, cold when we are warm, but most important, it keeps the yelling out. Lately my Mama and Dad have been fighting a lot more than usual. I'm kinda used to it now, because its been going on for so long. Sometimes I tell Aidan stories about what it was like before they fought. He doesn't remember because he was too little. I tell him about how happy Mama and Dad were and how much fun we all had. I make up most of the stories, because I honestly don't remember a time that Dad and Mama didn't fight. I tell him that this will end soon. But I don't think that's going happen. See, my Dad is a great handyman. He can fix anything, but something really big has been broken here and I don't know if he can fix it.

Aidan looks up at me with his crossed eyes and whispers, "Pashawn?"

Strange thing is, I know what he means. Ever since "D-Day" the yelling has stopped. That was the day they sat Aidan and I down in the kitchen and told us they were getting a divorce. I hate the word divorce so I call that day, "D-Day". Since then Aidan won't change out of his black and white Dalmatian pajamas and striped mittens. But worse, he has stopped using real words. All he's said since is "Pashawn", "Pea" and "Sashawn". It's a made up language that Mama says "He invented because he can't find the words to express how he feels." Maybe I'm the only one who understands him because I know how he feels. I know, because I feel the same way too…lost.

The past two weeks have been weird. Day by day, more boxes filled our house and Mama and Dad have been fighting a little less than usual. I told Aidan that it's because Dad is quietly planning a way to win Mama back, waiting for the right moment to say the right things and save our family. I want to believe this; I have to believe this and now's his only chance. I point my telescope back towards them as Dad pulls Mama in close.

He says, "You know it's not too late. I can get everything off that truck right now."

I yell out to Aidan.

"He says it's not too late! It's working Aidan!"

Aidan begins to chant.

"Pashawn, Sashawn, Pashawn."

I look back and Dad wipes a tear off Mama's cheek and leans in. That's it Dad, that's it. He's going for it, the big move. Come on Dad! Their faces are practically touching. They're about to kiss.

"Hey are we done here?"

I hear one of the fat, sweaty movers grunts as he steps between them. No, no, no. Don't interrupt them. Mama tries to look around the sweaty mover to Dad.

"Yeah, we're done."

"No!!!!" I yell.

Mama and Dad turn towards the fort. I duck down, hoping they didn't see me. I wait for a few seconds and then slowly peek up and out through my flower box. Mama and Dad have turned back and are talking to each other again.

"It's best for all of us." Mama whispers.

"You're right. We did our best." Dad says.

They both stand there, just staring at each other until Mama hands him the hula lamp and the hula girl's skirt falls off.

Mama screams,"Hula Heather!? Thank goodness you didn't lose your coconuts!"

They're both start to laugh.

Strange, just as my whole world is falling apart, they are having a chuckle-fest. Maybe they are right, that it is for the better, but I still think it stinks.

"Pashawn, Sashawn…"

I realize that my brother is still chanting.

"Stop. It's over." I say and he looks up at me with those

huge, brown eyes. I'm his big brother, I'm supposed to protect him, but I can't save him from this. I crouch down by his side and sigh,

"We lost."

He tucks his little head into my shoulder and he doesn't have to say anything, because I know how he feels. You don't need a made up language to cry.

Our fort is quiet for what seems forever. I look around it, trying to take pictures of everything with my mind. It's like a list, so that where ever we're going, I can rebuild this place.

"Okay you guys." I hear Mama yell from outside. I jump up and grab "Tommy" and tuck him under my arm.

"It's time, my little bears." She calls again.

"Do we have to leave?" I yell back.

I hear the wood steps on the rope ladder squeaking.

Mama pokes her head into the fort, "May I come in?"

Aidan doesn't even look up from my shoulder as I nod, giving her permission to come in.

"This stinks! You can't make us go." I say.

Like she always does, she just tilts her head and gives me that "look". Not an angry look, but an "I've-been-reading-books-on-how-to-deal-with-this", kind of look. I know what this means, she's gonna want to have "A Talk."

"This isn't fair! What about my plants, our fort, our school? Do you know what happens to new kids at our school? They get "Chilled". Yeah, that's right. No one speaks to them for a month. It's like they are a ghost and no one is allowed to break the rule. I heard some kids go crazy. Like Rupash. He was sent to the nut house!"

My Mama sits down on the floor across from us. She

crosses her legs and speaks in a soft voice, like the librarian uses when she reads the kindergarteners stories.

"Rupash didn't go to the nuthouse, honey. He moved to India with his family. I bet the new school will be great and I bet they don't even know what "Chilling" is."

I snap back "They probably have something worse."

I just glare at her. What does she know, she has no idea what it's like to be a kid now. She went to school like 50 years ago, she didn't have the pressure of trading cards, cyber-bullying or even "Call of Duty", which I am still not allowed to play and get teased about daily.

Mama puts her hand under my chin.

"Listen, everything Dad and I do is for you two. Your Dad and I need this change so we can be better parents. Things aren't working here for us anymore. We've tried. Really tried. But this is what we have to do. Although the house and the school will change, we are both desperately in love with you two and that, I promise, will never change."

Somehow in the middle of her speech, I found myself curled up in her arms. Her voice is calming and safe. She turns my head and looks me right in the eyes and says,

"You know everything is going to be okay, because you two are my everything."

Why is it that my Mama knows exactly what to say at exactly the right moment? I look over at Aidan and he's looking back at me to see what I'll do. This is big brother time. If I freak out, so will he. So I do what a big brother should and suck it up, wipe the tears off my face and try to smile.

"Can I bring Tommy?" I ask squeezing Tommy's flowerpot tight with both hands. It's all I can say because I'm having trouble holding back the crackling in my voice.

"Well it wouldn't be home without him, would it?" she says and I force an even bigger smile. She can say whatever she wants, but wherever we're going, I'll never call it home.

"Hey guys, the ship's leaving!"

I hear my Dad call from outside, like a ship's captain. He always does that when we are going somewhere.

"All aboard!" he yells like we are going on summer holiday.

"Aye aye Captain!" I yell back.

I spring to my feet and before I remember where it is we are going, I'm already down the rope ladder and have hopped up on to my Dad's back. Guys aren't like Mamas. We have a different way of talking. It's like we can take the emotion out of whatever is happening and just state the facts. My Dad pulls my legs tight around him, so I'm giving him a piggyback hug. "Be good and listen to your Mama."

I may be a guy, but I'm only eleven, and I can't stop the feelings that start taking over me. He can feel my body shaking as I try to hold back "The Big Cry", the one I hid from Aidan and he spins me around so I'm facing him.

"Look at me. Every other weekend is ours, just the boys."

Aidan runs over and holds on to Dad's leg. He hoists him up too and we are sitting in his arms like a basket.

"Everything is gonna be okay." He says and I nod my head, but he knows how much this is hurting us. I know he knows, because his eyes are red and his voice is shaky. "Only fourteen more sleeps, Aidan."

I think it's all getting to be too much for him, because he sets us down and pretends like he has something stuck in his eyes.

"Cailum, you're now the man of the house. You take care of Mama and Aidan. I'm only a phone call away…"

I don't want to hear anymore so I cut him off.

"I love you Dad."

He pretends he has more stuff in his eyes and wipes them as he says, "I love you too."

Aidan is trying to be strong and suck it up like I did, so he doesn't look at Dad. I think that if he did, he'd lose it, so he just looks at the street and whispers,

"Pashawn Pea."

Dad bends down and looks at Aidan.

"Pashawn Pea." he says back.

Aidan looks up at Dad, surprised. He's never used Aidan's language before and like I thought, he loses it, but so does Dad. He kneels down on the ground and holds Aidan in his arms.

"Time to roll, Mister!"

The fat, sweaty mover says, as he sticks his head out of the huge moving van. My Dad gets up and looks at us and puts his fist under his chin, pushing it up, telling us to "keep our chins up". He walks over to the van and hops in the passenger side and leans over the sweaty mover to honk the horn. Aidan and I don't wave, because we don't want to say goodbye.

As the huge moving van slowly pulls away, I see our crummy old station wagon, hidden behind it. Great, Dad gets all the good stuff and we get stuck with Old Rusty, our wood-sided station wagon. The old junker is loaded inside and out with luggage and stuff tied to the roof. My Mama slams the back gate shut and the back bumper falls off. She struggles to pick the heavy piece of steel off the ground but can't.

She sees us watching her.

"I think this can stay right here. It was weighing us down anyways." Just like her, making the best out of a crummy situation.

"That's all we are bringing?" I ask, because I don't see much furniture.

"Don't worry" my Mama says. "I have all your stuff and as for the rest, well, our new place comes fully furnished. Come on. We got to shake a leg if we're gonna get Old Rusty to Peterborough by morning."

My brother and I stuff ourselves into the packed back seat and roll up the windows because Rusty always backfires when she starts, leaving the car surrounded in a huge puff of smoke. As Old Rusty fills the air with an extra special, goodbye, cloud of smoke, I look out my window to see my house for one last time. I look at the house, the fence, the fort, the gardens... hold on! I have to blink a couple of times, not because of Rusty's smoke, but because I can't believe what I'm seeing. All of the flowers that the mover trampled now stand straight up with their bright colors shining in the sunlight. For a moment I swear I see them all bend over and tip their petals at me, like they are bowing. I hear a soft voice whisper,

"They're waiting for you."

I look down at Tommy and at the same moment, he too is bent over.

"Mama did you just say something?"

"No. Would you like me to?" she asks and then softens her voice. "Honey, this isn't the end, it's the beginning of a new adventure."

"Forget it." I tell her.

This must be some kind of daze caused by the fumes puffing out of Rusty. I rub my eyes and when I open them, we have turned the corner and I can no longer see my house.

(the second scroll)

The strangest thing has started happening to me when I'm falling asleep. My body becomes stiff and I can't move it and no matter how hard I try, I can't even move a finger. The only thing I have control of are my eyes, so I'm stuck there, frozen, looking around my dark bedroom and that's when I feel it. A heavy, dark feeling washes over me and I start to panic. Sometimes it comes through the door, sometimes through the window, but mostly I feel it coming from my closet, or from under my bed. I can't see it, or hear it, but I can definitely feel it, and it's evil. It usually circles me for a few seconds before I feel it come up to my bed. I try to yell, but nothing comes out of my mouth. I fight so hard to yell for my Mama or Dad, but I can't and it suddenly becomes hard to breathe. I feel the" bad thing" pressing down on me, like it's sitting on my chest and it's really, really heavy. I close my eyes and wiggle hard to make myself move. I start talking to it in my head, telling it to leave, that I'm not afraid of it, but I am. I fight so hard to move that my body gets covered in sweat. Sometimes it lasts for minutes and sometimes it lasts for hours, but it always ends the same way. As fast as it comes into my room, it leaves and suddenly I'm able to scream. I kick my covers off and sit up in my bed; my body shakes from fear and being soaked with sweat. That's when my parents come running into my room and try to tell me it wasn't real. My Mama says that where she comes from they call it "The Old Hag" and people have been having this happen to them since the olden times. She says it's just a dream. I looked it up on the Internet and it says that the scientific term for it is Sleep Paralysis. They say it happens when our minds wake up, but our bodies are still asleep. It wasn't always like this. It never used to happen to me, but ever since Mama said we were moving, it happens every time I go to sleep. So for the last two weeks I've been trying hard to stay awake, but I can't stay awake forever.

I try to lift my head away from the car window but my pillow is stuck to my face with drool. I must have fallen asleep. Wait…I fell asleep! No "Old Hag" this time. YES!!! I guess Mama's singing must have done the trick. Old Rusty hasn't had a working radio since I was 5, so Mama sings campfire songs whenever we go on long drives. It's always the same songs: "Ninety-Nine bottles of Pop", "Quarter Master Store", "The Ship Titanic" and "The Old Army" song. I don't know why, but she still laughs every time she sings, "They say that in the Army the beans are mighty fine, one rolled off the table and killed a friend of mine!" That's funny, a giant bean. It's been a long time since I slept for more than an hour or so and as I start thinking of how big a bean must have to be to crush someone, I start to drift off to sleep again.

"OW! What was that for?"

My brother punched me hard in the arm.

"Aidan, we called truce on punch-buggy a long time ago." I say, struggling to open my eyes and rubbing my arm.

"Pashawn!" He gasps.

Usually I only hear my brother gasp when there is a new mod available for Minecraft, so I crack my eyes open and look out the window. Our car has stopped and I don't know where we are. Mama opens her door and gets out of the car. She walks up to a pair of large, twisted gates that look like ivy and have flecks of purple paint peeling off of them. Mama tries to open them. She pushes with all of her strength, her face turns red and I can hear her squeal, like when she lifts a sack of potatoes up onto the top of the fridge, but the gates don't budge. She stops pushing and stares at the gates, then winds up and kicks them. It must really hurt, because she hops around holding her foot and saying words that I know we would get a consequence for even thinking about. All of a sudden, there is a loud, cracking noise and Mama jumps back from the gates. Both sides of the huge, twisted gates swing open. They make a long, high pitched squeaking sound, sending big, black crows flying out of the trees and into the foggy air. When the gates are fully open, Mama dusts her hands off and scolds the gate as if they can understand her.

"That'll teach-cha, you old trouble makers!"

She then walks back and hops into the car, calm, as if this happens everyday.

"Where are we?" I ask.

"Well, good morning sleepy head." She says, "It's an old shortcut I know."

Now in any movie I've ever seen, people who take shortcuts end up getting lost.

"I'm okay with taking the long way." I say.

"Don't be silly" Mama replies and we slowly drive through the gates.

I look back and as we pass through the heavy old gates they close behind us, all by themselves!

"Mama! The gates just closed!"

My mama looks at me in the rear view mirror and says calmly "Of course, sweetie. They can't keep out unwanted visitors if they're left open."

I lean forward and whisper to Mama, so I don't freak out Aidan.

"Those gates just closed all by themselves!"

"It was probably some kind of spring and pulley thing. You don't expect people to have to open and close those heavy gates by hand, do you?" Mama whispers back.

I sit back and keep my eyes forward, too scared of what else I might see if I look back, as Old Rusty slowly moves on. Our old station wagon rattles as her wheels creep over the dull, purple stones that cover the long driveway. I try and look as far ahead as I can, but I see no end to the bumpy road. It twists and turns, back and forth, disappearing into a dark forest. I reach down onto the floor of the car and pull my newest invention out of my knapsack, a pair of binoculars. Actually, it's two toilet paper rolls taped together with yellow glass from a vase Mama broke, taped over the ends. The yellow glass makes darkness seem brighter and everything I see around here is very, very dark, so I raise the binoculars to my eyes and look through them. On both sides of the road there are creepy, overgrown, grey gardens. The fields all around the gardens are overgrown with long, dead grass that sways in a mysterious fog. Rows of twisted trees line the sides of the road and scraggily, grey bushes, that have no leaves, run behind them like a fence. I look around the wide, dead fields and deep into the dark gardens, trying to find any sign of a living plant, but all I see are lifeless grass and empty branches. What happened here? Was it some kind of tree disease? Maybe it was a fire, set by some teenagers, making everything dead and grey as charcoal. Wait! What was that? I point my binoculars towards the dead bushes that run behind the trees. There they are again! Through my binoculars I see strange shadows scattering back and forth behind the twisted tree trunks. They seem to appear and disappear into the bushes, keeping up with the speed of our car. They can't be shadows cast by the trees or bushes, because it's barely light out, so there is not enough sun to even make shadows. I watch them for a few moments, trying to figure out what is making them, are they some kind of reflection off our car, a thick kind of fog? Did I just see that? Yep, I did. OMG!!! Those aren't shadows. Those are things! Those are "Shadow things" that have eyes! Big, glowing, yellow, cat-like eyes!

I pull my binoculars away from my eyes and check the yellow glass on the ends of the tubes for smudges. Aidan is always touching my stuff and he always has sticky fingers. I check the glass closely, but there isn't a single smudge. Okay, calm down Cailum. It's been a rough day. I am pretty tired, so this must be my imagination. Dad says I have an overactive one, so that's probably it. My heart is beating like a million beats a minute. I take some deep breaths and try to slow it down. Come on, I know that wasn't real, how could it be? Shadows with glowing eyes, pffft, whatever. Wow, not getting enough sleep really plays tricks on your mind. It's all in your head…but just to be extra sure, I'll look through my yellow glass tubes again. You know, double check so I don't end up having nightmares tonight. I lean over Aidan and check his side first. Just as I thought, there's no sign of them. I sit back and point my binoculars out my side… just as I thought…THEY'RE RIGHT THERE, Shadows with glowing yellow eyes, scattering behind the trees just like before! One of them turns and looks straight at me and I hear a growling voice in my head say, "We've been waiting for you."

Suddenly, all the Shadows stop moving. They all turn, look right at me and then all at once come flying towards the car. I drop my binoculars on the floor and close my eyes. Any second now I'll hear the "thud" as the Shadows hit the car, trying to get at the person who saw them. Me. Wait for it…wait for it…where are they? I should have heard them by now. Maybe they're gone or maybe they're just waiting for me to open my eyes. But I won't. I keep them shut tight. I know it's a trick and

I won't fall for it. Okay, this is taking too long. I think keeping my eyes closed is starting to freak me out more than looking at their glowing eyes. Not knowing where they are or what they're doing is making me sweat. Okay, that's it. I'm going to open my eyes. Yep, on the count of three, one, two…just then I hear it! Not a thud, but a long, grinding creak. Strange, I expected a louder sound. Those Shadows were flying at the car really fast, but they must have circled the car a few times and slowed down, just to tease me. I bet it was the sound of their nails scratching at the window. It doesn't matter though, a creak will do, cause I'm not the only one who's getting tricked. My Mama had to have heard that and it will totally freak her out. She'll realize how weird this place is and we'll have to turn around and go back to our old home, so the joke's on them.

I open my eyes slowly and whisper to Mama, "Did you hear that?"

I lean forward so she can whisper back, but she doesn't. She's gone! I turn and ask Aidan where she is, but he's gone too! I start digging under blankets and boxes in the back of the car, it's packed so tight there's no way they could be back there. Dad told me to take care of Mama and Aidan, my first job as "Man of the House" and I failed. What do they want with us? What if they took them to some horrible place and turned them into Shadow People? I have to save them! I look outside to find my best route to escape, so I can run and get some help. There is no way I'm going back towards those gardens again. Mama said this was a shortcut, so if I keep going straight I'll get to wherever she was heading. I stuff my binoculars into my backpack and put it on. I tuck Tommy under my arm and grab the door handle tight. Go! I throw open the car door and start running, following the direction of the headlights. They only shine a few feet into the thick fog and soon all I can see is a wall of milk white. The ground is lumpy and I keep tripping, but every time I fall, I get straight back up. Mama and Aidan need me and I'm their only hope. I have no idea what direction I'm running in but keep moving. I may not be able to see, but maybe that means the Shadows can't see me either. The ground gets flat and I pick up speed. I start sprinting…BANG! I slam into something and fall back onto the ground. I look up and standing over me is a tall Shadow.

"Cailum?" it whispers.

"AHHHHHHHHH!!!!!!" I scream and jump up.

I try to run and it grabs a hold of my backpack. I struggle to unclip the strap that holds it on around my waist, but it's stuck. I hold on to Tommy tight and swing my free fist into the fog, hoping to hit the Shadow monster. I may be eleven, but I'm not going down without a fight. I turn around, the Shadow moves closer.

"Ow." I hit it.

"You punched me in the leg!" it says, but that's no monster's voice…it's my Mama.

She lets go of me and rubs her leg as she moves close enough for me to see her.

"I'm sorry, I thought you were a monster."

I explain and she gives me that angry look.

"Clearly, the only thing to be afraid of out here is you."

"Didn't you hear that screeching noise?" I ask.

Aidan pops out of the fog to see what's happening.

Mama sighs, "Yes I heard it. I know, I know, you don't have to remind me. I have to get Old Rusty's squeaky brakes fixed. I'm sorry I left you in the car. I would have told you that we were coming out here, but your eyes were closed. We thought you were asleep and after all the trouble you've been having with "The Old Hag" lately, I thought you could use some good shut eye."

I feel horrible. Was I asleep? Was this just another visit from "The Old Hag?" Oh, man, what is happening to me? My nightmares must be getting worse.

"I'm really sorry Mama." I say. I kiss my hand and touch her leg.

She smiles. "Well that makes it feel better. Thank you. Well, now that we're all here…" She starts to limp into the fog,

"Follow me. I want to show you something."

I keep close to her, still afraid of what might be out there.

"Where are we going?" I ask Mama.

She takes a deep breath and says, "Home."

(the third scroll)

Not long ago at Queensbury, my old elementary school, this new kid, Keaton, had just finished his month long sentence of getting "Chilled". He'd survived without ever cracking, so I thought I should throw him a bone and sit with him at lunch. Even while he was being "Chilled", he was a cool kid and although they couldn't talk to him, all the girls whispered about him on the playground. They talked about his expensive clothes and the blonde streaks in his hair. Now that his "Chilling" was over, I had to beat the girls to him, so I could find out how he survived being "Chilled". It was a couple of days after Mama had told us we were moving, and I thought Keaton might have some tips on how I could survive my new school. I asked him how'd he do it? He laughed and said, " I've had worse. My family travels a lot and we move at least once a year. I've gone to eight schools in the last six years, so this was nothing. The only place I really know is our house in L.A., but I'm only there in the summer." I asked him if his Dad was in the army? He just laughed again and said, " I wish. My Dad's an actor. We're only here because he's shooting a movie." I Googled his name when

I got home that day and he wasn't lying, his Dad is really famous. Really, really famous... like, "face on your t-shirt" famous. The next day at lunch I sat with him again. I said, "I bet you can't wait to get out of this crummy town and go home to L.A.?" He looked at me and asked "Home? You think L.A. is my home?" I tried to blow it off "No, whatever, right?" We sat eating our sandwiches for a couple of minutes and then I tried to dig a little deeper, "So, where is home?" He looked at me as if I was nuts and said "Home isn't really a place." I think he could tell by the look on my face that I didn't understand so he kept talking. "Dad's always working, so he's never really around much. My Mom sets up the houses in every place we end up. She brings the same set of bed sheets to every place we end up in, so that I have something that's familiar. She's the one who makes my lunches and tucks me in most nights." He smiled, "So, I guess what I'm trying to say is, home isn't a place for me...home is wherever my Mom is."

We walk for a minute or two through the thick fog, but with Mama by my side I'm not as scared. Suddenly the wall of fog ends and we step out onto hard ground. It's made of the same dull purple stones as the road we were on and comes to an end, just in front of us, at the bottom of a hill. Large steps made of stone lead up from the loop at the end of the road to the top of the hill.

"There it is." Mama says.

At the top of the hill is the biggest, weirdest house I've ever seen. It's made up of stone and wood, with a tower on top. If Dracula's castle were built by Dr. Seuss, then this is it. The bottom of the house looks like a tree trunk and branches poke out of the mansion. No matter where I look, I can't see a straight line anywhere on it. The windows and doors are all odd shapes; no two of them the same and the porch that sticks out from the front of the house is so bent that it looks like it's made of wet noodles. Mama walks up to the top of the hill and turns to us.

"That was sure a long ride. Anyone gotta pee?"

Aidan starts running up the stairs, but I just stand there, frozen, still staring at this enormous, eerie house.

"Cailum", Mama says "Are you sure you don't have to go?"

Suddenly a terrifying scream comes from the thick fog behind me and I jump. I hear a rustling coming from the garden in the middle of the loop. I don't know if it's a squirrel, a snake or a skunk, but I'm not sticking around to find out.

"I guess I should at least try!" I yell and without a second thought, shoot up the stone stairs towards Mama.

"Home Sweet home" Mama says as she opens the large, wavy glass door and it creaks just like you think a scary old door would.

"There is nothing sweet about it." I say under my breath.

"What are you talking about?" Mama says. "It's a little dusty, but with some elbow grease, it'll feel like home in no time."

We step in and it's as weird as the outside and twice as huge. There are cobwebs everywhere and everything is covered in grey sheets. The ceiling must be a hundred feet tall and strange paintings of old women hang on the walls. I swear there is at least an inch of dust on everything, including the floor and as I step into the enormous front hall, each step I take causes a puff of dust to fly up into the air. I'm allergic to dust and cats so I begin to sneeze out of control. Mama reaches into her purse and gives me an allergy pill.

"Sorry baby. We'll get all this dust cleaned up before you know it."

I click the light switch off and on, nothing happens.

"Really, Mama?"

She always sees the bright side of things, but this place has no bright side, the lights don't even work. I can't believe she thinks this house of horrors is okay.

"This place is awful." I tell her, "I mean, who used to live here? The Boogie Man?"

She looks at me startled, "The Boogie Man?"

Has she lost her memory as well as her mind?

"Yeah, Mama, you know. The Boogie Man."

Her face turns white.

"Hides in your closet. Says boogie, boogie, boogie. It's a joke, Mama"

She lets out a little giggle and says, "Don't be silly. Of course the Boogie Man never lived here...I did."

"Pashawn. Sashawn?"

Aidan almost falls over he is so shocked.

Mama turns and nods. "This is Kokotilo Manor. It's been in my family for many generations. This is where I grew up..."

"Wait a second..." I stop her, " You mean you own this place...we own this place?"

Mama nods again.

"We're rich! Lets just sell this creepy old place and buy a new one! I can get a dirt bike!"

Mama sighs, "It's not that simple. We aren't rich. Yes,

Kokotilo Manor is big, but I'm not allowed to sell it. It's our family's home; it's always been our family's home and always will be. Look, I know it doesn't look that great now. It has been closed up for a long time, but when I was your age I thought this was the most magical place in the world. I know you boys will grow to love it too. Just give it a chance. It's all in how you choose to see it and believe me, you ain't seen nothin' yet!"

Mama runs over to the huge, twisting staircase at the end of the front entrance and skips up the stairs! This is so unlike her. Mama never skips.

"Come on Boy-o's!" She yells as she reaches the top of the stairs. "I'll show you my old room."

I look at Aidan, "She's kidding right?"

Aidan looks at me and shrugs "Pashawn Pea?"

"Your wrong." I tell him "There is no way this is her old house. She's just trying to make us feel better about it."

Mama yells again, "Last one upstairs is a rotten egg!"

As bad as this place is, neither of us wants to be a rotten egg.

Aidan raises his eyebrow "Sashawn?"

I give him a cold stare and say, "You're goin' down." I get ready to sprint. "On your marks, get set…"

Aidan takes off.

"False start, false start." I scream, but he is already at the

32

bottom of the stairs and isn't stopping so I take off after him.

At the top of the stairs we suddenly stop, both of us don't want to take a step further. The hallway is empty and long. It's darker than downstairs and honestly I'm scared.

"Tied?" I ask Aidan.

"Pashawn." He nods back.

I yell into the dark hallway, "Mama?"

From far down the hall we hear her voice. "I'm here."

Aidan grabs my hand and we take a few careful steps forward. There are crooked doors on both sides, all the way down the hallway. More paintings of old ladies fill the spaces between the doors.

I hear Mama's voice again "Sorry about the lights boys. The power won't be on until tomorrow."

As Aidan and I pass the first crooked doorframe, a Shadow scampers out from under the bed and disappears into the closet.

"AAAAAHHHHHHHH!!!" Aidan and I yell at the same time and run away as fast as we can. I see a flickering light coming from a room on the right, just before where the hallway splits into two. We sprint towards it and when we reach the doorway, I see Mama and dive into the room.

"Whoa, whoa. What's wrong?" Mama asks.

Out of breath and so terrified I can barely speak.

33

"Something was…was in the…under the…bed. It ran into…the closet."

"It was probably a mouse." she says calmly.

I look at Aidan and he's shaking. I remember what Dad said, about being the man of the house and I try pretending it's nothing.

"A mouse. Yeah, of course a mouse. Right Aidan? Old house equals mouse. Simple. No big deal. I was just teasing you. Boy, if you could have seen your face."

Aidan shakes his head "No" and Mama says again, "It was a mouse."

Aidan looks suspicious, "Pashawn?"

"Yeah, it was a joke." I smile but Mama is not impressed.

"Don't scare your little brother."

" Sorry" I say.

Mama pulls out a pack of matches from her pocket and lights another candle. Now the whole room glows with light. Wow, unlike the rest of the house this room is actually pretty. There is a fairy thingy hanging from the ceiling and one of the walls is covered with a painting of some kind of fantasyland. All the other walls are covered in posters of old rock bands. I guess having long hair and wearing make-up was cool for guys in the 90's. The dresser and chairs are made of twisted wood and it's painted in white paint that sparkles. In front of the huge window

34

is a giant bed. It looks fluffy and soft, but mostly it looks bouncy. My eyes open wide. Mama smiles at me.

"You wanna?"

I smile back. "I think we have to."

We all run and jump onto the bed. The ceiling is so high, we can all jump as high as we want and not bang our heads. Mama, Aidan and I jump up and down, giggling. Most times we play together Mama usually stops, but this time she doesn't; she just keeps on jumping and laughing. Maybe this place is magical. Maybe we are all under some spell, but whatever it is, I hope it lasts, because I don't ever want Mama or Aidan to be sad anymore. I think we all have had too much of that over the last few weeks, so we just keep on jumping.

For the first time in the history of playing with parents, I'm the first to tire out. I flop down onto the soft bed, Aidan follows and Mama falls between us. It's a classic snuggle and one I think we've all been needing.

Mama says, "We never had that much fun at the old house did we?"

She kisses us on the forehead and climbs out of the bed. When she reaches the door she turns to us.

"So there is nothing to worry about, there hasn't been anything under the bed in years."

She grabs a candle off the dresser and walks out the

door. Aidan and I lay frozen. Did she just say what I think she did? She must have just messed her words up. From the dark hallway I hear her call, "Can't lay there all day. Come on, I'll show you your new room."

As her voice fades I hear a growl.

"Did you hear that?" I ask Aidan.

He nods and we both jump to our feet, standing side-by-side in the middle of the bed. I hear the growl again. It's coming from under the bed.

I grab Aidan's hand and whisper, "When I say, jump as far from the bed as you can."

We begin to bounce up and down on the bed. On the third bounce, we jump as hard as we can and land on the floor. I don't turn around to check how far away we are from the bed, instead I grab Aidan's hand tight and head for the door.

Once again, I'm running at top speed down the hall, chasing flickering candlelight. I haven't run this much in one day since I had hiccups in Mrs. Slangly's gym class and she made me do laps every time I hiccupped, because she thought I was making noises on purpose. Way down at the other end of the hall I see the candlelight coming from an open door. When we get to the doorway we slow down and walk in, like nothing happened, so we can avoid having another one of her "Talks". This room is much more dusty than Mama's room. There are old wooden toys scattered all over the floor and against the far wall there is a humungous bunk bed. It's posts are made of trees and the ladder is made of vines and twigs. Mama walks over to the large window and opens the curtains. What little sun can peek through the thick fog fills the room with grey light.

"This used to be my brother's room." Mama says.

"Brother?" I ask. "Mama, we didn't know you had a brother."

Mama turns away from us and starts brushing the dust off of the toys.

"Oh I'm sure I have mentioned him. You boys never listen. If it's not in a video game, it's in one ear and out the other. I know I told you about Uncle Marty."

It's weird, Mama won't look at us, instead she just keeps tidying the room. She used to do this when she didn't want to talk to Dad. There is a really long silence. I know she never said anything about a brother to me and by the look on Aidan's face, this is the first time he's heard it too.

Mama clears her throat "Don't just stand there. I think you boys have a decision to make."

She nods at the bunk beds.

"Who's going to take the top bunk?"

Her words are like a starter gun going off and instantly Aidan and I race to the vine ladder. As I try to climb the ladder,

Aidan pulls me off and I fall to the floor.

"Boys!" Mama yells, but we keep going.

He's halfway up the ladder, so I grab a wooden toy and chuck it at him. He leans to the side to dodge it and loses his grip and as he hangs to the side, I see my opportunity and I pass him on the ladder. As I reach the top I feel his hands clamp onto my shoulders. I dive over the wooden edge of the top bunk and Aidan holds on for dear life. We fall onto the top bunk at the same time, but my body touches the mattress first.

Mama yells again.

"Boys! Stop! If you can't solve this peacefully than no one gets to sleep on the top bunk."

I fling Aidan off my back and get ready to rumble. I was on here first and he knows it. I reach out to grab him, but he rolls out of the way. Wait a second. He rolled out of the way? That's when I notice just how huge this top bunk is. It's as big as two of my parents' beds put together. Aidan and I peek over the edge of the bed. I look down at the bottom bunk, way down. I can't help but think of the growl we heard in Mama's room. It and the Shadow we saw in the first room both came from under the bed. I can't make Aidan sleep down there and I sure am not gonna do it. I look at Aidan and he has that "please" look in his eyes.

"Well boys? What is it going to be?" Mama says in her angry voice.

"I think there is enough room for both of us up here." I answer.

Mama has her hands on her hips and says nothing, but raises her eyebrows, not buying it. I have to work fast to convince her.

"Mama, he's only eight and this divorce thing is really freaking him out…also, if Uncle Marty comes to stay, he can have the bottom bunk."

Mama smiles. "That's very sweet boys. You can both sleep on the top bunk, but no rough housing. You can save the bottom bunk for one of your new friends…Marty won't be coming to visit."

She picks up an old teddy bear and looks sad.

"We haven't talked in years."

She brushes the dust off of the bear and puts it up on the shelf, then starts cleaning again like she does when she doesn't want to talk, but I do.

"Where is he?" I ask.

Mama ignores my question "We should get Rusty unpacked. All the cleaning supplies are underneath the boxes. Can't have you sleeping in a dusty room, can we Sneezy?"

She suddenly stops tidying and just walks out the door.

"What was that?" I say to Aidan. "Why won't Mama tell us where he is? Why didn't she ever mention him before and why did she lie?"

"Pashawn" Aidan says and holds his hands out like criminals do when they get handcuffed.

"You think he's in jail? Maybe. All I know is, the last time Mama all of a sudden stopped talking about someone was when Minky died."

Aidan eyes widen and I'm pretty sure I know what he's thinking. I lean over the edge of the bunk bed and look around the room. Unlike Mama's room that had posters of rock bands and other teenage stuff, Marty's room only has toys. We pull back from the edge of the bunk.

"He hasn't been here in a very long time." I tell Aidan. "Maybe Mama didn't tell us where he is, because she doesn't know. Maybe he is hiding. Remember when you were five and we used to play hide and go seek? Where was your favorite place to hide?"

Aidan's voice shakes. "Pashawn."

"That's right," I whisper back. "You always hid under the bed. Do you think the ghost of Marty is hiding under the bed?"

Aidan and I peek over the edge of the bed again. Now my voice shakes. "Only one way to find out Aidan." I try to swallow, but my mouth is suddenly dry and my voice squeaks as I call out, "Marty…come out, come out, wherever you are?"

(the fourth scroll)

Just after I turned eight, Minky showed up at our house. Dad found him hiding in the woodpile. He tried everything he could to get the cat to leave, but no matter what he did, it just kept coming back. Dad isn't much of a cat person; maybe it's because I'm allergic to them or because he says they are lazy and can't hunt duck. Everyday it kept hanging around and soon something about that little kitten got to my Dad. He started leaving bowls of milk and cans of tuna out for him. Dad said, "His fur was as soft as mink" and he stopped calling him "cat" and started calling him Minky. My Dad was right, his fur was soft and best of all, I could rub my whole face in his fur and it didn't make me sneeze. When it got close to winter and the weather got really cold, Dad built him a little house. It had carpet inside and a flap to keep out the cold. By the time the snow came, Dad couldn't bear the thought of Minky outside so he brought him into the house. We all loved him, but he was kind of Dad's cat, he followed him around the house and slept on his pillow every night. When spring came and Dad was working in the yard, Minky was right by his side. He went everywhere with my

Dad and acted more like a dog than a cat. He came when you called him and Dad even taught him how to shake a paw. One day, Dad was digging in the garden and like always Minky was right at his side. Suddenly, he jumped to his feet. Dad loved the hunter in Minky and kind of talked to him like he was a hunting dog. "What is it Minky?" he said. Minky's tail started to sway slowly back and forth. "Ready" Dad said. "Go get em!" Minky took off and that's when Dad saw what it was that Minky was after. It was a squirrel on the other side of the road. I heard the loud engine revving down the street. Dad yelled out "Minky stop!" Minky wasn't like other cats; he listened to my Dad and stopped right there in the middle of the road. That's when the car hit him. It didn't even stop. I can still remember the sound of the car screeching as it drove away. My Dad ran over to help him, but it was too late. My Dad was so angry that he broke the shovel he was digging with in half. He picked up Minky and carried him back, like he was holding a baby. My Dad doesn't cry; he gets "stuff caught in his eyes" and when he buried Minky in the garden that night, his eyes were full of stuff. My

Dad and I talk about a lot of things, but we never spoke of Minky again.

I reach over Mama to look at the clock, it's 3 A.M. I've never stayed up this late in my entire life. I always thought that adults stayed up late because there was something awesome that would happen after kids fell asleep. Like after they tucked us in they'd have a party or watch a scary movie kids aren't allowed to see. Well, this sure isn't a party and if it's a scary movie, I want it to end. All night I've been thinking about Minky and Dad…and Marty. Aidan and I were too scared to sleep in the bunk beds, so we convinced Mama it was a good idea to sleep with her. I told her that Aidan was the one that was scared and since he was going to sleep with her, I might as well too, just to make him feel better. I don't want Mama to know I'm scared. It's my job to take care of her and Aidan. I keep looking into the dark, watching for Shadows, watching for Marty.

Even though Mama is beside me I feel alone, I'm the only one awake in the whole house. Even Tommy has gone to sleep. His leaves are all curled up because of the cold air. I hold him tight under my arm. I know it's silly, like a plant is going to protect me? Maybe Marty is allergic to tomatoes, but even then I'm pooched, because Tommy won't sprout fruit for a couple more months. I hear a growl.

"What was that?" I whisper, but I'm the only one awake to answer.

"There it is again!" I look deep into the darkness, but

nothing is moving. Oh no. Is it under the bed? I clutch Tommy tight and I shift over to the edge of the bed. Slowly I dangle my head down off the side. I close my eyes. It's okay, if I see something, I'll scream and then Mama will wake up. Here I go…I open my eyes quickly…nothing there. I whip my head back up. Where is that sound coming from? Where is Marty? Think Cailum, think. What would I do if I were a kid? Wait, I am a kid. I get it; he's just playing with me. Teasing me.

"Okay then Marty. You want to play…let's play."

I hear the growl again.

"Ahhhhhhhhhh!" I yell.

Mama rolls over and mumbles, "What is it honey?"

She's still half asleep. The growling happens again, but this time I know where it's coming from. It's my stomach. Being terrified hasn't helped my appetite and I really haven't eaten much since yesterday.

"Nothing Mama." I whisper. "Just talking in my sleep."

She must not be all that worried about me, because she is already snoring. Oh man, my stomach is killing me. I'm tired and hungry and honestly I've had it! This is stupid. An eleven year old afraid of the dark! No way. Not me. I'm the man of this house and I'm hungry, and when a man is hungry he does something about it! I'm gonna go downstairs and make myself a snack and that's, that! But first, I need to get out of this bed and avoid whatever "isn't" hiding under it. I may be the man of this house, but I'm not crazy.

I don't know what has come over me but suddenly I feel brave, strong…fearless! I look at the open door and study my path of escape. There is a chair beside the open door with a fluffy cushion on it and an old rug on the floor between the bed and the chair. I wiggle over to the edge of the bed, being careful not to wake Mama and Aidan. I take a deep breath and as I breathe out, it's as if everything goes slow motion. I launch myself into the air, pushing really hard with my legs, so that I get as far away from the bed as I can. I stretch my arms out in front of me and balance Tommy on my fingertips. I look back and the bed is getting further away from me and I'm starting to fall towards the ground. I flick Tommy with my fingertips and he flies end-over-end through the air, landing safely on the chair's soft cushion. I bend my neck backwards and arch my back. I land softly on my chest and shoot across the floor using the old rug like a toboggan. At the last second I snatch Tommy from the chair and tuck him under my arm as the rug comes to a sudden stop. I tuck my knees up and flip through the air, out the door and land on my feet in the hallway.

Like a spell has been broken, the slow motion feeling goes away and I realize how impossible what I just did was. I'm not a super hero or a stuntman; I've never even taken gymnastics.

None of this makes sense. "How did I do that?" While I'm trying to understand the impossible acrobatics I just did, the pain in my stomach takes over. I guess nothing stands between a man and his meal.

"Whatever is out there..." I puff my chest out and say in a deep "manly" voice. "Better stay outta my way. Cause this Man's gonna do, what this Man's gotta do, to get me some eats!"

It's a long way down to the kitchen and this house is even freakier at night. I stayed awake so long keeping watch in Mama's room, that my eyes are adjusted to seeing in the dark. It's a good thing too, because the whole way down to the kitchen was pitch black. We've been here for a full day now and this is the first time I've even stepped foot in the kitchen; maybe that's why I'm so hungry. Even in the dark this kitchen looks like it jumped right out of Hansel and Gretel. There are wooden cupboards lining the walls that look like they were carved by hand out of whole tree trunks. At the far end of the kitchen there is a fireplace made of stone that's taller than I am, as wide as old Rusty and I bet you could cook a whole cow in it and still have tons of room. It looks like the fireplace I saw on the field trip to the "Pilgrim's Village." All that's missing is an old lady in old-fashioned clothes stirring the giant pot that hangs inside it. Wait. Forget that. I really don't want to see an old lady suddenly standing there. The thought of that just freaked me out. "Old

Timey" costumes always do, so I turn away from the fireplace. As I try not to look at the fireplace I notice that the ceiling is covered with bunches of dried flowers, weeds and herbs. Some of them I recognize from my plant books, others I've never seen before. A few of the flowers hanging from the ceiling look like the ones in Mama's garden at our house. Even dried and dead they still have kept their strange colors and shapes. Wow, this place just keeps getting weirder. It may be weird but it worked because the thought of the old woman is pretty much out of my mind, so now I can "get down to business."

On top of a large, old wooden table I see the bag of groceries Mama brought. My mouth starts to water. I dig through the paper bag and pull out everything I don't want; can of beans, can of mushrooms, can of corn, bag of Mama's favorite rice crackers, a bunch of Aidan's grapes...jeez, is there anything in here for me? If I don't find something soon, this is gonna be one gross bean-mushroom-corn-grape-rice cracker sandwich! I set Tommy down on the table so I can stuff both my hands back into the bag and dig down to the very bottom. "Please, please, please!" I feel something, flat, smooth, not quite the shape I'm looking for, but maybe it's something good. I grab it and pull it out.

"Fail!" It's a tiny box of Aidan's cereal. I look at the crummy food laid out on the table.

"This stinks!"

As usual, Aidan gets all his favorite stuff and I get pwned! I turn around to yell up at Mama and just as I am about to yell, I see another paper bag, over on the counter. "Cailum" is written on it in black marker and around my name there are little hearts. I run over to it and look in. Bingo, it's all there, everything I need for my favorite snack!!! One by one I pull them out; bread, peanut butter, banana and butter. I've done this a thousand times before at home, Dad showed me how. I see a stack of heavy black pans piled beside the fireplace, so I grab one and put it on the stove. I butter the outside of two slices of bread and put them in the pan; they begin to sizzle right away. I then spread the tops of each piece of bread with peanut butter and I make sure it's good and thick. I cut thin pieces of banana with a butter knife and place them on top one of the bread slices. Then the final step. This is where most beginners mess up and just put the other piece of bread on top. The secret is to squish them together with the flipper. This makes the flavors mix together and makes it easier to stuff in your mouth.

"Ta-Da!" A fried peanut butter and banana sandwich! Dad said that these were "The King's" favorite sandwiches. I'm not sure what he was the king of, but he must not have had a lot of guards because Dad told me he died on the throne. To honor him, Dad and I always say a cheer before we inhale our snack.

So even though Dad's not here, I raise my sandwich high into the air, snarl my lip up like Dad taught me, and speak in "The King's" native language.

"This her Isa Hunka-Hunka, Burn'n Samich!"

I've made a lot of F.P.B.& B's before, but I think this one is the best. I plunk myself down on a chair at the table and try to chew slowly, so I can enjoy every delicious mouthful. It's so good that at first I think I'm starting to see stars, but then I realize it's just the reflection coming through the kitchen window and bouncing off the glass of some old doors. I didn't notice them when I first came into the kitchen, but the reflection of the twinkling star is so bright that both doors are now all lit up. I grab Tommy, tuck him under my arm and I walk over to the doors. As I get closer, I see that the handles look like leaves and the glass is divided by climbing vines. I push my face up to the glass and try and see what's on the other side, but it's so dirty I can't see a thing. I take the last bite of my F.P.B.& B and pull one of the heavy doors open. I don't believe what I'm seeing; an entire room made of glass, brightly lit up by the star and a full moon twinkling in front of me. I look at Tommy tucked under my arm, and whisper "I think we found you a home."

I can hardly catch my breath as I step down the glass steps and into the room. It's like someone climbed into my head and pulled out the plans for my perfect greenhouse. Every detail is exactly the way I'd want it. This is not your grandma's greenhouse; there is nothing "dainty" about it, and everything in it looks thick and sturdy. There are rows of handmade pots that spiral up twisted wooden racks, potting beds made from giant stones running down both sides and even the air is the perfect temperature and moisture, making it feel as warm as a spring night.

In the middle of the greenhouse there is a giant tree; it's trunk is as wide as a house and it has to be at least a hundred years old. It's branches spread out across the glass roof of the greenhouse making amazing shadow shapes on the ground. The very top of the tree pokes out of the glass dome in the middle. It fits so perfectly; it's like the greenhouse had been built around it. I walk around the tree's enormous trunk and hidden behind it, along the far wall, are a bunch of cabinets. They are stacked one on top of the other, forming an arch at the top. I can't resist knowing what awesome things are hiding behind the dirty glass, so I run over and open them. The bottom one is packed full of glass bottles filled with brightly colored liquids, the one above it has glass jars of strange seeds and the cabinet above it is filled with even stranger shaped bulbs. Every cabinet I open has more of the same strange liquids, seeds and bulbs in it. The last two cabinets at the top of the arch are too high for me to reach, so I set Tommy down, and drag over a heavy pot to stand on. I have to go up on my tippy toes to reach the cabinet handles, which seem to be stuck. It's probably just rust or something, so I give them a good yank. Suddenly they open, throwing me backwards and I fall onto the floor. I lay there for a second, checking to see if I broke anything. Leg...good. Arm...check. Head...still on. Just as I try to stand up, something falls out of the top cabinet and hits me so hard that it knocks the wind out of me. As I stand up, I see what hit me. It's a large, heavy book. I pick it up and set it down on the stone table under the arch. The cover looks like it's made of birch bark and the spine is held together with green vines. There is a thick layer of dust on the cover and when I let go of the book, the dust where my hands were falls off and I notice something is burnt into it. I plug my nose and blow hard to remove the rest of the dust and under it, burnt, brown letters appear. "C...A...I...L...U...M."

"Cailum." I hear someone behind me say and I jump, knocking the book onto the floor.

"Are you okay? I didn't mean to scare you." It's Mama.

I'm glad it's her. For a second there I thought it was the Shadow again.

"I'm fine." I tell her, but I know I must be as white as a ghost. I look around and it's no longer night. I've been so focused on the cabinets I didn't notice that the greenhouse is filled with sunlight.

"What time is it?" I ask her.

"6:30" she says.

How could I have been down here for three hours? Did I get knocked out when I fell off the pot? Was I dreaming? I look down and see the book behind my feet, poking out under the stone table. I don't know what happened to the time but the book is real.

"Did you leave something in here for me?" I ask her.

"No." she says and I can tell by the look on her face she isn't lying. Who left it here then? Is this a Marty thing? I don't want to scare her too so I try to brush over it.

"I just thought…you might have…you know, Surprise! New house…gift!"

She isn't buying it.

"That is a huge tree." I say changing the subject and making her look up, so I can push the book completely under the table with my foot.

"Yes it is." she says. "I knew you'd like it in here. It's almost magical, isn't it? I used to spend hours in here when I was about your age. Trying to create new flowers and plants. I guess you inherited my green thumb."

"You think?" I ask.

"I got mine from my Mama." She says and now she's the one who changes the subject. "We should get going. There will be lots of time to play in here. We've got a big day ahead of us."

She turns and walks towards the doors.

"I'll be right there," I tell her.

"Okay, but hurry, I don't want us to be late for your first day at your new school." she says as she walks out the doors.

"Oh, crud!"

With all the craziness going on I forgot we were going to the new school today and now that Mama has seen me, it's too late to fake being sick. I don't know what's worse; this house of Shadows or getting "Chilled" at a new school. I hear Mama yell from the kitchen over the banging pots and pans.

"What do you want for breakfast Cailum?"

"I'm good." I yell back. "I just ate."

I am actually pretty full from that F.P.B. & B, and it'll also buy me a few more minutes alone in here. That book has my name on the cover and I have got to see what's inside. I look around the tree and out the doors to see if Mama is watching me. The house may have changed but Mama sure hasn't. She's doing the same thing she does every morning. She's busy running back and forth getting breakfast ready and making lunches. She has her humungous 1980's headphones strapped to her head and her old school "walkman" clipped to the belt of her robe. I can hear the heavy metal music blaring from all the way back here. For such a gentle person, she listens to some very hard music.

Unless a bomb goes off, she won't notice anything, so the coast is clear.

I get down on my hands and knees, fish the book out from under the stone table and sit down on the floor. I open the heavy book and on the first page there is some kind of strange writing.

I stare at the symbols on the page, trying to figure out what they mean. Is it some kind of code? A riddle I'm supposed to crack? Out of nowhere, a warm wind blows and flips the book closed. I hear a soft whisper, like the one I heard when we drove away from our house.

It says, "Look again."

Who said that? None of the glass windows in the greenhouse are open and Mama is still busy, running back and forth, rocking out in the kitchen. I hold the book tight in my hands, so no wind can blow it closed again and open the heavy bark cover. I look down at the first page and the symbols have changed into letters!

> "Now that you are almost,
> twelve years old,
> it's time that the truth,
> was finally told.
> There are things all around us,
> that few choose to see.
> Magic exists Callum,
> and you hold the key,
> Safe from the shadows,
> and bumps in the night,
> The magic's kept safe,
> hidden far from their sight,
> These pages lead,

to where magic is found.
Begin by making beauty,
grow out of the ground."

Who did this? How could this old book have my name in it? Then I remember that Mama said that she "knew I would like this place." Nice try Mama! I do have to give her points for the disappearing symbols; they must have been written in some kind of invisible ink or something. I put the book on top of the table and leave it open to the first page. That way she will see it and know that I'm on to her. I turn around and start walking out of the greenhouse. Wait! What was that? Out of the corner of my eye, I swear I just saw a Shadow moving beside me! Not my shadow. One of "those Shadows"! I turn slowly to my right and there it is! I stop and it stops too! It's eyes begin to glow bright and it looks angry. I'm not waiting around to see more so I run out of the greenhouse and slam the doors shut, locking it inside! I lean back against the doors, terrified. Not of that Shadow, it's trapped in the greenhouse. The real horror is outside somewhere…waiting for Aidan and I and there is no way to escape it…it's our new school!

to et šo

(the fifth scroll)

When I was in grade three, our school did a Christmas play called "Angels and Lambs, Ladybugs and Fireflies". The grade 7 and 8's got all the good speaking parts and the 5's and 6's got all the human parts. The animal parts went to the grade 4's, grade 1 and 2's got the tree parts and the grade 3's got the bug parts. I got stuck playing a grasshopper. Overall it wasn't that bad, at least I wasn't made a ladybug like Derrick. To this day his nickname is still ladybug, which is cute if your mom calls you that, but doesn't look good on the back of a hockey jersey. Being a grasshopper was cool with me and all I had to do was hop down the aisle at the end and sing the last song with everyone else. Actually, I didn't even have to sing, I just mouthed the words. Everything was going great until my Mama decided that she was gonna make my costume.

She made it out of a little girl's green bodysuit that she got from the secondhand shop. It covered me from head to toe. It had a hood that was so tight it squished my face up like a raisin and the rest of it was stretched so much that you could see right through it. Mama added green and brown wings to cover my " less than Christmas appropriate" areas. I'm not sure how many wings a grasshopper has, but I know the twenty dangling felt flaps were way too many, not to mention the odd diaper of felt that drew more attention than I really wanted "down there". It took three of us to get me into the "green suit of embarrassment" and once I was in it, I could barely move. I tried to tell Mama that I didn't want to wear it, but she looked so proud of the costume, I didn't want to hurt her feelings. The night of the performance I decided to suck it up and just bury myself into the middle of other bugs; that way no one would see me. I told myself "It's just one song. Mouth it and it's over." When the music started, I hid behind the bleachers at the back of the gym and took off my robe. As the groups of bugs passed I waited for my chance and when a group of locusts came by, I wiggled myself into the middle. Just as we were stepping out onto the carpet, Mrs. Ducain grabbed me by the shoulder, "No grasshoppers with the locusts, they are mortal enemies!" As she pulled me out of the group, she started to giggle. "Well, well. Your mother must have worked very hard on this costume. I'm sure she will want to get a good picture of you." She told the locusts to go, then turned to me. "Such a special costume deserves a special spot. You get to go down on your own!" She then pushed me out into the gym. I started to make my way down the aisle, walking as fast as I could and Mrs. Ducain yelled from the back "Hop! Hop! You're a grasshopper!" As I started to hop up and down in the tight suit, Kenny, an eighth grader who was head of the AV club, shone the spotlight right at me. Everyone was staring at me and with every hop, I heard a tiny ripping sound. I started to hop faster, because the sooner I made it to the stage, the sooner it would all be over. That's when Kenny shone the spotlight right into my eyes. There was no way I was slowing down, so I closed my eyes and just kept hopping. I knew from rehearsal that once I reached the end of the carpet, it was only a couple of hops across the gym floor to the stage stairs. Practice makes perfect, but I never practiced with the "green suit of embarrassment" on. I had no idea how slippery the spandex covered feet were gonna be on the shiny gym floor. As soon as I took my last hop off of the carpet and my feet touched down, they shot out from under me and I hit the floor right in front of everyone. Dad always says that the show must go on, so I tried to hop back up to my feet, but when I did, again my feet slipped out from under me and I fell back down. Four or five times I tried to stand up; each time I fell down and as I did, the audiences' "oooo's" turned to "aaaahhh's" and Mr. Pike started playing the piano faster, like in an old movie. Finally, I jumped up and my feet stuck. I turned away from the audience and began to hop up the stairs, but as I reached the stage I felt a strange cool breeze. The audience behind me burst into laughter and I realized the suit was no longer tight. I looked down and saw that the whole suit had torn apart and rolled up around my neck like a scarf, leaving me standing there in my undies. I dove into the group of locusts and as the show went on, I quietly crawled off the back of the stage. Since then I stay out of the spotlight and always wear clean underwear.

The new school looks like a prison with it's tall towers and stonewalls. There are stone gargoyles on either side of the front steps and weird carvings of knights and monsters on the walls. Above one of the doors it says "Boys" and above another door it says "Girls". Mama said that in the olden days, boys and girls had separate entrances and even separate classes. Now they are all mixed together and I'm trying to avoid them. When the recess bell rings and all the kids go out to the playground, I make a break for the bathroom. So far, so good. I've made it a third of the way through the day and I haven't been "Chilled". Maybe Mama was right. Maybe this school doesn't do that? But even if that's true, I'm laying low and not bringing attention to myself, just in case they have something even worse here. I poke my head out of the bathroom and look both ways down the hall. Empty. Then, out of nowhere, this girl appears in front of me.

"You're the new kid, right?" she asks.

I'm not sure what to say, so I just look at her. I don't spend a whole lot of time looking at girls, but this girl is really pretty. She's waiting for me to say something, but I just keep staring. Now I feel weird.

"Can you like, not talk or something?" she says.

Now I know she thinks I'm weird too. I better say something.

"I can talk." I blurt out and she just stares at me.

I start to sweat.

"I can also do this with my fingers." I say and as I twist my fingers into the shape of a cobra, I realize how nervous I am and how really crazy I am acting. Why am I showing this stranger…this pretty stranger the cobra fingers? This is my first day at school, this is the first person that's talked to me, my first words to a very pretty girl and this is what I say? What's wrong with me? Oh man, I deserve to get "Chilled".

The girl looks both ways down the hall, then grabs me by the shirt and pulls me into the boys' bathroom.

"No, you're a girl, this is the boys' potty." I blurt out. What am I doing? Potty? Great, now they are all going to call me "Potty."

She puts her hand over my mouth, "Shhhh. I know you're the new kid, so here is a heads up. Everyone is going to P.U. you. Just ignore it, like it's no big deal. If you do that, it'll only last two weeks. But if you break, there is no telling how long they'll keep it up."

I pull her hand away from my mouth, her really soft hand that smells like flowers.

"What is P.U.?"

She pinches her nose and says, "They are going to plug their noses and pretend you smell."

She lets go of her nose, leans in and takes a whiff of me.

"You don't smell. Actually, you smell pretty good."

She turns to walk out.

"Wait, why are you telling me this?" I ask her. There is no good reason for her to tip me off, unless of course, she's setting me up.

She turns and laughs, "Because I heard you moved into the weird house on Fourlorn Street. That place is older than the town. I'm sorry to be the one that has to tell you, but it's haunted. None of the adults believe it, but all the kids in town know it's true. Most won't even walk down the street, but I have and I've heard the strange noises coming from behind those old purple walls! So you're parents are either rich or crazy or both. Whatever your story is, I figure you've got enough to deal with at home, so I thought you could use a break."

She looks at me close.

"So, are your parents rich?"

I shake my head.

She smiles. "Just as I thought, crazy."

I smile back, "Thank you...uh?"

"Rachel" she says and walks out.

Rachel. Rachel. Raaaaaay-Chaaaal. The pretty girl who thinks I smell pretty good.

Just like Rachel said, the rest of the day all the kids plugged their noses when I passed and just like she told me to do, I pretended it didn't bother me. After school I wait for Aidan by the jungle gym. It's far enough away from the front doors that I don't have to deal with all the kids P.U.-ing me. Rachel comes out of the school and I pretend like I don't see her, but she obviously sees me. She starts walking towards me and as she passes, she plugs her nose and I hear her whisper.

"Nice job today. Keep it up."

I know she had to plug her nose; if she didn't the other kids would P.U. her too. I really don't care, because she didn't have to give me the heads up or take the risk of talking to me now, but she did.

"Pashawn?" Aidan is standing in front of me, wearing his puppy pajamas and mittens.

"I can't believe you wore those to school. At least take the mittens off." I tell him and he just shakes his head no.

"How are we supposed to make friends with you dressed like a Dalmatian?"

Aidan just shrugs his shoulders.

"Well, did you get P.U.'d?"

Aidan smiles "Pashawn, Sashawn, Pea?"

"You know, did the kids in your class plug their noses and pretend you smell?"

Aidan shakes his head no again and a group of kids run over and high-five Aidan one by one as they pass. One of the kids turns around and says;

"Don't forget to turn on your computer when you get home so we can play co-op."

Aidan nods, "Pashawn."

Another kid shouts "Later Doggy Dude!"

I stand there stunned. "Great. I do everything I can to avoid drawing attention to me and everyone pretends I smell. You wear puppy pajamas to school and get an online play date."

The walk from the school to our new house isn't that far, but my backpack has a full year of textbooks in it, so it seems like it takes forever. As long as it takes us, it isn't long enough, because Aidan and I eventually end up in front of the giant, purple ivy gates.

Aidan stops and stares at them, "Pashawn."

I've been dreading this moment ever since Mama told us that she wasn't going to be picking us up after school. There is no way around it. On either side of the gates are faded, purple stone walls. The house is at the end of the long road and on both sides of that road are those creepy gardens. Mama told us this was the shortcut…I'd hate to see the long cut. Through the gates and up the driveway is the only route we have.

"Sashawn." Aidan says with a shaky voice.

"I know, Aidan. Me too. But we'll just have to gun it. Here, give me your backpack. When I open the gates, run like there is free candy at the house."

Aidan hands me his backpack; it's lighter than mine, but still has a few books in it. I sling it over my shoulder and walk up to the gates. I try to pull them open but they don't budge. I look back at Aidan and he pulls the hood of his pajamas up on his head. The doggy ears on the hood stand straight up and he nods at me to go ahead. I pull my foot back and get ready to kick the gates like Mama did, but suddenly the giant gates squeak open, all by themselves. Aidan growls at them. His pajamas may make him feel like a fearless dog, but I've got enough fear for both of us.

"RUN!" I yell.

Aidan takes off through the gates, barking. I run as fast as I can, trying to catch up to him, but the backpacks are so heavy and he just keeps getting further away. He rounds a bend up ahead and I can still hear his barking, but I can't see him. I hear all sorts of noises coming from the dead gardens on both sides of me. The cracking of branches, high screams and deep dark growls get louder and louder as I get further up the road. I see a large Shadow pop out from behind a huge, twisted tree trunk up ahead. Then other Shadows begin to pop out of the gardens all around me. I dig deep inside and gather all the strength I have. I let out a loud yell, like a war cry, and then something inside me explodes and I take off like a rocket up the road. In seconds

I round the last corner and suddenly I am neck and neck with Aidan. We both shoot up the hill and reach the wavy front steps at the same time and burst through the front door. I chuck the backpacks on the ground, slam the front door shut and Aidan and I collapse onto the floor.

"Hello my little bears." I hear Mama say.

I look over and see her walking out from the kitchen. She looks at us lying on the floor, huffing and puffing, trying to catch our breath.

"What's wrong? Why were you running?"

"There's...something...in...the bushes." I say, still trying to catch my breath.

Mama kneels down beside us. "Slow down. What's in the bushes?"

"Shadows." I tell her.

"Shadows?" she asks and I can't stop myself from spilling the beans.

"Yeah. In the gardens, under the beds, in the greenhouse..."

Mama's face changes, she doesn't look like she's listening, she looks concerned, scared almost. If she gets scared, then who do we have to protect us? Dad isn't here and so far the Shadows seem to go away whenever we are with her. If she is scared, does that mean we won't be safe when we're with her anymore? I can't take that chance.

"Fail!" I pretend to laugh. "You should have seen your face! You so fell for it. I wish I had that on camera, that would get like a million hits on the internet and gone totally viral!"

I elbow Aidan and he looks at me confused. I give another nudge and he pretends to laugh too, but he isn't very convincing.

"It was just a race Mama and Aidan won. He sure is fast. We bet that the winner would get a cookie."

Aidan may not like lying, but he does like cookies, so he smiles at Mama.

"Congratulations, Aidan." Mama says, "But you two shouldn't scare me like that."

Aidan looks at her sad.

"Ah, go on into the kitchen and get yourself a cookie." she says.

Aidan runs into the kitchen and I try to follow but Mama stops me.

"Tell me about your day. How was it?"

"Fine." I tell her.

"Did you make any new friends?" she asks and I shake my head no. She holds my head still and looks into my eyes.

"Did you try?"

She doesn't know how hard it is to make friends. She holds my head and gives me that smile, the one she uses when she wants to talk. I don't like where this is going.

"Can I please go now. I don't really feel like talking. I... want to hang out in the greenhouse for a little while...alone."

She lets go of my head and steps to the side so I can pass. As I walk away, I turn back and see Mama looking at me, with a sad look on her face. There are a lot of things I can take, but my Mama being sad isn't one of them.

"Rachel" I say.

"Rachel?" she sounds surprised.

Maybe it's because it's a girl's name or maybe it's because I can't help but smile when I say it.

"Yeah. Rachel."

Mama's face lights up.

I open the dirty glass doors to the greenhouse and look around for the Shadow. I see no sign of it so I go straight for the stone table, where I left the book. When I round the big tree I see that the book isn't there.

"Gee, I wonder who could have taken it?" I say sarcastically and turn around, expecting my Mama to be walking in any minute.

I wait a few seconds, but she doesn't walk in. I pull the giant planter over again and climb up on to it. I open the top cabinet and "What do you know?" there it is. I pull it out and climb down. I wonder what she has written in it now? Boy, I can't believe she's gonna keep this mystery thing going. I grew out of scavenger hunts when I was like, five. I open the heavy bark cover and there is nothing on the page. I flip through them all but they're all blank. What's the deal? This isn't much of a scavenger hunt if there are no instructions to follow. Oh Mama. Classic beginner mistake, writing the whole thing in invisible ink only works if I read it right away. Whatever. I tried.

I close the book and put it back in the cabinet. I climb down and as I start to walk out of the greenhouse, I am stopped by a loud noise. It sounds like breaking glass and it's coming from the cabinets. I walk slowly back towards the sound and as I get closer, the cabinets start shaking. Suddenly, one of the doors opens. Bottles of seeds fly out and smash on the floor. Then the door above it opens and some dirt spills out. One by one the doors open from the bottom up, until the only one left is the one with the book in it. I climb up on the planter and reach up to undo the latch on the cabinet door. BANG! The door swings open and I am thrown off balance. I have to flap my arms in the air to stop myself from falling. Just as I get my balance, a Shadow shoots out of the cabinet and hits me in the head. "Wait a second," I think as I rub the sore spot where the Shadow hit me, "Shadows aren't hard." I quickly turn and see the Shadow scamper across the floor, dragging…the book! What does Marty's ghost want with a book my Mama made…unless

Mama didn't make it! "Holy fish crackers!" I hop off the planter and run after it, but before I can even round the tree, he flies up and out one of the open glass panels in the roof.

"Not funny, Uncle Marty." I yell. "You better bring it back!"

Or what? What am I going to do to a ghost? What's worse than being dead? Nothing. So, there's nothing I can do but watch as he disappears into the dark garden with my book.

(the sixth scroll)

I was always afraid of our basement. It was damp and smelly and something about it gave me a real creepy feeling. Even when I was down there with Mama, helping her fold the laundry, I didn't feel right. It wasn't the water heater that rattled, or the stairs that were just boards, or even the darkness; it was the feeling that something was watching me, and "it" knew that I knew it was there. My Dad is big on chores and one of mine was my to get the ice cream at the end of dinner every night. It was stuffed in the bottom of an old freezer, way back in the farthest corner of the basement. Since I had to go down there every night, I decided to make a deal with "The Thing" that lived down there. In my head I told "The Thing" that I had until the count of ten to get down the rickety old stairs, run across the cold, concrete floor, open the creaky freezer, get the ice cream, close the freezer and get back up the stairs. If I couldn't do it by the count of ten, then "The Thing" could get me. So every night, when dinner was over, I'd stand at the top of the basement stairs and flick on the light. I felt like "The Thing" was hiding under the stairs, waiting to see my feet, hoping to grab them either on my way down or up and drag me away to somewhere awful. I'd take a deep breath and then yell out:

"1..." I'm running down the stairs...

"2..." leaping off the bottom step, just missing the hot water tank...

"3..." running across the cold concrete floor, so fast I don't know if my feet actually touched it.

"4..." I open the creaky freezer and...

"5..." dig down deep trying to fish out the ice cream, but...

"6..." it's buried under new stuff Mama bought on grocery day, so it's really hard to find.

"7..." Run! The heavy freezer lid slams shut behind me.

"8..." I only look up so I don't see "The Thing" hiding under the stairs.

"9..." I'm only half way up the stairs and now I'm sure I'm a goner.

"And a half...!" As the words come out of my mouth, I can almost feel "The Thing's" hands on the back of my ankles.

"10!"...I'm standing at the top. I made it. It's over... until dessert tomorrow night. And that's why I hate ice cream.

All night my mind has been racing, thinking about Marty and the book, about Shadows in the garden, but for some reason, I've been mostly thinking about Rachel. What is it about her that makes my mind go in circles? Her hair? Her eyes? Her hands? Was she going to kiss me in the bathroom before I went and ruined it by doing the cobra hands? Will she ever kiss me? I've never thought about anyone kissing me before. Am I good enough to kiss? OMG! I don't know what's happening to me. It's like I've been put under some kind of girl spell. If you put a microphone in my head right now, all you would hear is "Rachel, Rachel, Rachel, Rachel…" How am I ever going to get through today without making a complete fool of myself?

Mama lets Aidan and I out in front of the school. There must be a couple of hundred kids on the playground, but of course my eyes instantly fix on you-know-who. She's standing over by the trees, talking with some girls. The girls see me staring, point at me and then plug their noses. Rachel plugs hers too. It's not exactly the greeting I was dreaming of all night for, so I pick up my backpack and walk towards the doors. I hear someone call Aidan's name. It's one of the kids he met yesterday. Aidan runs over to them. Even if I'm being "P.U.'d" it's good to see him smiling. Ever since Mama and Dad told us about the divorce, I've been really worried about him. At first I understood he was upset, but it's been months and he still hasn't snapped out of it.

He's still wearing the same puppy P.J.'s and mittens and talking in a made up language. I was worried that maybe he'd never be the same again. But there he is smiling and laughing, running around with these new friends and I feel a little better, because I know my little brother, my best friend, is still there inside him, somewhere. Maybe this place isn't so bad, it seems to be doing good for Aidan. I lift my head up, ignore the kids plugging their noses and walk into the school, ready for what ever else they can throw at me.

Our teacher, Ms. Flunkan, stands at the front of the class and puts a painting smock on over her matching tracksuit. It's our art period and she clearly has something against it.

"Lets hurry up and get this artsy fartsy garbage over with." She yells.

She pulls out her shiny silver whistle and blows it. This is only my second day, but I'm beginning to understand this is her way of communicating with kids; she blows first, asks questions later. She blows her whistle again and all the other kids in class raise their hands. All the kids look at me and Ms. Flunkan yells.

"Ah Kokotilo, you're the last to put your hand up, so you'll have to go get the art supplies from the art supply room."

Whatever, so I have to go get some art supplies. Ha, ha jokes on me. I'm not gonna let them think this bothers me, so I stand up and say,

"No problem. Where is it?"

Ms. Flunkan gives me an evil smile and says "The basement."

Oh, no. It all comes back to me; the ice cream, the water heater, the freezer, the stairs and "The Thing". After a few years of being terrified every night after dinner, I did a little research and was able to convince our doctor that I was allergic to milk. He told my parents I was "lactose intolerant" and Mama got rid of all the milk products in our house...including ice cream. I do miss cheese, but it's a small price to pay to not have to deal with "The Thing". Even though I've gone out of my way to avoid all basements since then, a bargain's a bargain, a basement is a basement and the deal with "The Thing" still stands. I've got ten seconds to get in and out or I'm his. I begin to sweat. Everyone in class is staring at me. Is this why they don't want to go to the supply room? Do they believe in "The Thing" too? Before I know it, the rough hands of Ms. Flunkan are on my shoulders, pushing me towards the stairs.

"You're new, so you get the instructions once. There are the stairs. Go down, turn right, then left, open the metal door, prop it open with the brick; if you don't you'll be locked down there till the janitor finds you. Pull the chain to turn on the light, go seven rows in and get enough construction paper for the whole class and then come up. Make sure you get enough paper or I'll send you right back down. Got it?"

She gives me a nudge and I start to walk down the stairs.

"Hurry up. We haven't got all day." she yells and walks away.

I can't tell where the stairs end because about twenty steps down they disappear into darkness.

"Left then right?" I try to remember.

"No. Right, then left. Brick…door, light, paper."

My palms get all sweaty and I realize there is no turning back. I'm the new kid and if I'm too scared to go down to the supply room, the other kids will never let me forget it. I make my sweaty palms into a fist and take a deep breath:

"1…" I run down the stairs.

"2…" The light fades as I go into the darkness.

"3…" I turn right.

"4…" I turn left.

"5…" I open the metal door and search around the ground for the brick.

"6…" There it is. It's heavy. It takes both hands to drag it over and prop open the door.

"7…" I pull the chain on the light and am no longer in the dark, but I have the strong feeling something is definitely watching me.

"8…" I run down the center aisle, past row after row of

art supplies, looking for the construction paper. Bingo! I stop at the seventh row. Both sides have shelves, floor to ceiling that are filled with construction paper. As I run down the right side, I see something move at the end of the row and I stop. It's a Shadow, a large Shadow and it's real. There is no time to deal with this!

"9…" I yell and I fill my arms with paper, but I know my time has run out. Maybe I can run faster than it? As I turn to run, for a spilt second, the Shadow changes its form. Although it happens as fast as a flash of lightning, I see it change from a Shadow, into a grey, wrinkled, thing with no teeth and tuffs of wiry white hair. I take a deep breath and…

"10…" I hear a voice behind me yell and I drop the paper. I look up and the monster is gone from the end of the row. How could it have gotten behind me so fast? My only option now is to fight. My terror turns to anger and I close my eyes, spin around and yell.

"BRING IT ON!"

"Bring what on?" I hear the voice ask.

I open my eyes…it's Rachel.

"Lemme guess, you gave yourself twenty seconds to make it in and out or "The Cellar Dweller" can take you?" she says with a smirk.

I'm totally embarrassed so I brush it off.

"Cellar Dweller? What are you talking about? I was just

counting how many pieces of paper I needed."

She sighs, "Really? So you always yell when you count?"

She raises her eyebrows and waits for me to answer, but like when we first met in the bathroom, I'm tongue-tied.

"I just came down in case you needed my help." she says. "Normally "The Cellar Dweller" doesn't come out when there is more than one kid down here. But I guess you've got it all under control, so I'll leave you alone to 'scream count' the rest of the construction paper."

She turns and starts to walk away.

"Ten" I yell and she stops.

I guess the fear of being alone has untied my tongue.

"I gave myself ten seconds."

"Amateur." she says and gives me a punch in the arm. "So, did he come out?" she whispers, like she's afraid of someone or something hearing.

"I think so. Grey and wrinkled…" I whisper back.

She looks around, "What? You saw him? No one's ever actually seen him, most of the time you can just feel him, watching you. One time I saw a shadow out of the corner of my eye, but you're the only one I know who has actually seen him."

She sticks her arm out, "Look, he's watching us right now. I can feel it."

Her arm is covered in goose bumps. "This always

happens when they're around…"

I stop her. "They? You mean you've seen…or felt others?"

She steps back from me, "Haven't you?"

Behind her a stack of paper falls off the shelf and bangs on the floor. She grabs my arm, pulls me in close and whispers.

"I really don't want to talk about it down here." She then mouths the words, "He can hear us."

She lets go of my arm and raises her voice.

"Lets just get the paper and get out of here. I told Flunkan I was in the bathroom and if I'm not back soon, she'll find us and we'll both get detention."

She starts loading my arms up with paper and I keep an eye out for the monster. It only takes her a few seconds to make a stack so high I can't see. She grabs onto one of my hands, underneath the stack of paper and leads me out of the basement. I have to carry the weight of the paper on one arm mostly, but I don't care, BECAUSE SHE'S HOLDING MY HAND! She tries to hurry me along, but I drag my feet a little and pretend I can see less than I actually can, so that I can keep holding on to her hand for as long as possible. I know that monster is down here, but a hand holding with Rachel may never happen again, so I milk it for all its worth. If "The Cellar Dweller" wants to take me, then take me now, cause after touching her soft hand, I have now lived.

Way too soon, we reach the top of the stairs and she lets go of my hand. She pokes her head around the stack of paper and says,

"This is where we split up. I'll go in first. You count to ten and then come in."

She walks down the hall and then says over her shoulder, "Just don't yell it this time."

to_ešo_eᴎo_et_šg

(the seventh scroll)

Phil Potts was a kid who lived down the street from our old house. He was an alright guy. He had cool toys; he loved to play guns and was a really good lookout for the fort. He didn't have any brothers or sisters and I think he was a little jealous of how well Aidan and I got along. For a while we all played great together, but that all changed when he started asking Aidan and I to make him a full member of our fort. We told him that only family could be made members, because my Dad built it just for us. He said he understood, but not long after that he began acting weird. He'd show up at the fort when Aidan wasn't around and when we were all together he'd make up games that only two people could play. He started calling me his "best friend" and used it at least once in every sentence he said. He also stopped saying Aidan's name and instead called him "your little brother" and really hitting the word "little" hard every time he said it. It got on my nerves and I know it hurt Aidan's feelings, so I decided I was gonna tell him to stop, the next time I saw him. One Saturday, before Aidan came outside, I went out to the fort to water my plants and have a little " me time". When I got up inside, I found Phil standing over by my workbench. The number one rule of our fort is no one is allowed to be in it unless Aidan or I are there. I told Phil he had to leave and that he had to stop calling Aidan "little" if he ever wanted us to play with him again. He said, "I'm sorry, but I wanted to get here before Aidan did, because I need to tell you something. You know how you are having trouble growing that plant?" He pointed to an orchid I had been trying to get to bloom, that was sitting on my workbench. He then looked me dead in the eyes and said, "Aidan's been poisoning it!" I called him a liar and told him to get out. "I saw him." he said and pointed to a bottle of bug spray that was hidden behind the couch. "I saw him pour it into the dirt." I grabbed the bug spray and walked over to the orchid. I pinched a little bit of the dirt, put it into my hand and smelled it. It smelled like poison. Just then Aidan climbed up the ladder and walked into the fort. Aidan and I have no secrets so I asked him, "Did you poison my plant?" He said no and Phil started to yell. "He did too. I saw him." I pointed to the door and said, "You better leave now Phil. I want to chew Aidan out in private." He slowly started to walk towards the door. "Thank you." I said. "You're a good friend. This will only take a second." I put my hand out to thank him. When he shook my hand I grabbed his with my other hand. I pulled his hand up to my nose." What do you know Phil? Your hand smells exactly like the poisoned dirt. Get out of our fort now." He yanked his hand back and pleaded, "That's because when I found where the poison was, I touched it and it got all over my hands. You gotta believe me. Go on, smell Aidan's hands, it's only fair." I looked at Aidan and he suddenly put his hands behind his back. "Aidan let me see your hands." He tried to look away but I walked over and stood right in front of him." Now Aidan!" He pulled his left hand from behind his back and held it out. "And the other" I ordered and he slowly held out his right hand as well. Under the smell of the oranges and toast that he had for breakfast, I could smell the bug spray. "Why would you do that?" I asked him and before he could speak Phil shouted, "See I told you. I'm your best friend. Not him. Kick him out of the fort." Aidan went to speak, but I cut him off, "I'm sure there is a good reason for it." Phil's face went red" What? You were going to kick me out when you thought that it was me who poisoned the plant, so now you should kick him out. Whose side are you on, your best friends, or your worst brothers?" I looked down at Aidan and his face was suddenly sad. I told him, "He's right, you know, it's either you or him..." Aidan turned and began walking out of the fort. Just as he got to the door I said "Well, goodbye Phil." Phil's mouth dropped and I grabbed him by the collar of his shirt and forced him over to the ladder. I made sure he'd climbed all the way down and then I pulled the ladder up. He looked up at me and yelled. "Come on. You're choosing that lying little runt over me?" I looked at Aidan and then back down at Phil and said, "Yep. I am." He looked at me completely confused and asked," Why? I'm your best friend!" I just smiled and said, "If you really were my best friend, you'd know to never make me choose between anything, or anyone and my brother...CAUSE I'LL CHOOSE HIM, EVERY TIME, NO MATTER WHAT."

Aidan and I raced up the driveway after school again today. At one point, as we rounded the second curve, I thought for sure that Marty's Shadow was gonna catch Aidan, but out of nowhere he did some kinda flying kick and the Shadow backed off. I asked him to do it again when we got to the house but he couldn't. Like the freaky flips I did jumping out of Mama's bed, this power of Aidan's came and went. It's too bad, cause that flying kick was rad.

As soon as we walked in the door, Aidan took off upstairs to our room. He wanted to play online with some of the kids from school, so I told him he could have our computer all to himself until dinner. To be honest, I'm glad he's out of my hair for a while. From the start, today has been full of all sorts of crazy surprises and I need a moment alone to sort them all out. I guess there is no better place to start, than the start; Marty's Shadow and the book he stole.

I walk into the kitchen and Mama's waiting for me. As I walk towards the greenhouse doors, she stops me. To my surprise, she doesn't say anything or ask me anything; she just hands me something wrapped in paper towel. She nods and I open it…Perfect! A fried P.B.&B., just what I needed. After Rachel holding my hand, which I still haven't washed, and seeing that ugly monster in the basement, I kinda lost my appetite for lunch. But now I'm starving.

"Thanks Mama, I really needed this." I say.

She winks at me and then just quietly walks out of the kitchen. Wow, what is going on today? Is there a full moon or something? She saw I was upset and she didn't even try and have one of her "Talks" with me. Well, I guess the surprises today just keep on coming.

I take a huge bite of my sandwich and open the greenhouse doors. I look around for a clue, any clue, anything that can tell me why Marty's ghost stole the book. Funny, that the same day he steals the book, I see a Shadow in the basement of my school. Marty's Shadow and the Shadow in the basement have got to be connected, I just need to figure out how. I walk over to the stone table and look around it. I open the cabinets and look in all the planters, but I can't find anything. I look through the glass walls, towards the dark forest that Marty's Shadow escaped to and wonder where he went. I see something move behind a tree, it's Marty's Shadow! I can see it's glowing yellow eyes watching me. I know I wanted to be alone so I could figure this out, but I didn't want to be alone with a dead kid's ghost! I slowly start to walk backwards towards the doors, hoping he won't notice I'm moving, until I'm close enough to make a run for it.

"Cailum can you take these crackers up to Aidan?" Mama calls from the kitchen. "You know how he gets if he doesn't eat."

Mama's voice is normally as soft as a mouse, but when

she calls for us, it's loud enough to wake the dead, for real. Marty's Shadow hears her and shoots across the garden towards me.

"Be right there." I yell to Mama.

The Shadow swoops up the glass walls and through an open pane in the roof. I start running backwards, keeping my eye on the Shadow, and trip over the edge of the stone planter that surrounds the giant tree. I fall back against rough bark and the Shadow suddenly stops, just feet away from me. I push myself up, using the trunk for balance. The Shadow wiggles like a snake in the air, up and down, back and forth, but doesn't come any closer. It starts circling the planter, round and round like it's waiting for me to make a move and when it passes behind the backside of the tree, I do. I jump off the planter and make a run for the doors, but the Shadow cuts me off. With nowhere else to go, I run back to the tree and again the Shadow stops at the edge. Maybe the Shadow isn't waiting for me to make a move, it's waiting for me to step away from the tree? I step away from the tree and the Shadow bolts towards me. I jump back against it and it stops. That's it. There is something about this tree that the Shadow doesn't like. Well at least I'm safe here, but I can't stay here all night. The Shadow keeps circling, round and round and I'm trapped.

"Cailum. I asked you to take these crackers up to Aidan."

Mama yells and steps down the stairs and into the greenhouse.

Instantly the Shadow disappears.

"Sorry Mama." I say and jump down from the planter. I run past her, snatching the plate of cheese and crackers out of her hand and take off through the kitchen.

"WOOF!" I hear a strange noise coming from upstairs. Oh no. The Shadow! Aidan's alone in our bedroom! I rush to the up the stairs and down the hall, but stop just outside our door. I recognize the voice coming from inside. It's one of the kids from school that's been hanging out with Aidan. They're talking online.

"Pashawn?" Aidan asks.

"No. Not that, do the other thing," a different kid demands. "Come on boy!"

There is a long silence and then I realize what the strange noise was. It's Aidan, barking.

"Again!" all the kids online shout and Aidan barks again, "WOOF.WOOF!!"

As he barks over and over the kids laugh. Not the good kind of laugh, the mean kind. I don't think Aidan understands, so he laughs too and that's when they start to tease him.

"SASHAWN, SASHAWN read all about it, Aidan's a dumb dog, no doubt about it."

I open the door and shout, "Stop teasing him!"

Instantly the kids online are quiet.

"Turn off the computer." I yell.

Aidan looks at me, embarrassed, but tries to cover it by laughing, so I close the lid of the laptop.

"That wasn't funny. They're teasing you, Aidan."

He shakes his head and looks at me as if I'm crazy.

"Look, I know it's hard to make friends being the new kids in school, but real friends don't treat you like that. They don't make you bark and they don't call you dumb."

He doesn't want to hear it.

"Sashawn, Pashawn, Pea!" He says and pushes me out of the way, knocking the tray of snacks out of my hand and storms out.

For the rest of the night he wouldn't speak to me. No matter what I said, he wouldn't believe that those kids were teasing him. The more I thought about it, the more I realized why he wouldn't want to believe me. Even before D-Day, he wasn't the most popular kid at our old school and with everything that's happened, having friends, even if they are teasing you, must feel better than being alone. But it still isn't right. I hate those kids for teasing him, but most of all, I hate that he might lose that smile, the one that showed me the old him was still inside.

At breakfast this morning, he wouldn't even look at me. On the ride to school he just looked out the car window and hummed, trying to drown out the sound of my voice, even when I wasn't speaking to him. Before old Rusty can squeak to a stop, Aidan opens his door and takes off into the playground. I kiss Mama goodbye and get out, watching him run over to the swings where the same kids I heard teasing him last night are standing. The bullies circle around him, laughing. Even from this far away, I can tell he's doing his fake laugh, trying to join in. As I walk up the stairs to the front doors, I hear Aidan bark. I stare at the bullies. I'm so angry that if they looked at me right now, I swear my eyes would cut them in half like lasers. One of the bullies taps another on the shoulder and they both stop laughing and point at me. Aidan turns around and when he sees it's me they are pointing at, he stops barking and gives me a "What" look. I keep giving the kids the evil eye.

"Pashawn!" Aidan yells at me, but I just keep staring at the bullies. The biggest one turns his back to me and I notice something. There is a Shadow clinging to his back! The Shadow looks at me and then suddenly the bully yells, "PASHAWN!"

The other kids start to laugh and join in the teasing.

"PASHAWN! PASHAWN!"

That's it! I drop my backpack and run towards the bullies. When I get my hands on them, they are gonna know not to pick on my little brother. But, just as I get close to them, the Shadow flies away and the kids suddenly stop laughing. They all just stand there dazed for a second and then the biggest bully says, "Come on guys, this is boring. Lets go." And they all walk away.

"Let's go Aidan." I say and grab him by the arm.

Aidan yanks his arm out of my hand and steps back. He shakes his head, turns away from me and chases after the bullies.

"You're welcome." I yell and walk back to the school doors, still steaming mad.

I reach the steps and pick up my backpack. As I throw it over my shoulder I see Aidan, surrounded by the bullies, making a fool of himself. There's nothing I can do to stop him. He won't listen to me but I have to listen the bullies' laughter, all the way to my classroom, echoing through the halls.

I missed most of math class worrying about Aidan. I'm going to have a mountain of homework tonight, but I don't care. Sometimes there are more important things than compound fractions. Actually, watching a pizza pop cook in the microwave is more important to me than math. All through class I wondered, what was that Shadow doing on that kid's back? Why won't Aidan listen to me? Why are those kids so mean? Somewhere between Language Arts and Science, I figured out what I need to do. No matter what I say, or anyone says, Aidan won't listen. He may be little, but he's stubborn and the only way he is going to see how crummy these kids are, is by me backing off and letting him figure it out himself.

The recess bell rings. I run outside and hide behind a group of trees across the playground. The trees are thick, so no one can see me, but I have a clear view of the swings where Aidan's bullies hang out. Even though I know he won't listen to me, I want to keep an eye on him, just in case things get out of hand. I see them coming. They're laughing and talking about Aidan.

"What a weirdo."

"Yeah, totally SLD."

"I think he's ESL with that weird language he speaks."

The big kid points to the stairs, "There he is. Let's make him bark again."

The big kid turns and I see the Shadow is again clinging to his back. The other kids turn to look at Aidan. Holy fish crackers! All the bullies now have Shadows clinging to their backs. Aidan reaches the group and they all start to chant.

"PASHAWN! SASHAWN! Read all about it. Aidan's a dumb dog, no doubt about it."

Aidan just stands there, laughing.

How come this doesn't bother him? The kids keep chanting as they move over the jungle gym. It's pretty far away from where I am, so I dig down into my backpack and pull out my binoculars. I focus on the bullies. They're still teasing him. I look at Aidan through the rose colored glass and I see it! Hiding high on his back is the reason the teasing doesn't bother him and why he won't listen to me. Wrapped around his neck is a tiny Shadow. I must not have seen it before, because without the rose glass of the binoculars, the Shadow blends in with the black on Aidan's Dalmatian pajamas. I sneak over to some bushes, behind the slide so I can get a closer look. Under the hood of his pajamas, the Shadow is covering Aidan's ears. No matter what those bullies are saying, he must not be able to hear it. Now that I'm closer, I point my binoculars at the Shadows on the other kid's backs. Suddenly, like when I was in the basement, the Shadows change. For a split second, they have hooves, horns and fur. They look just like...BULLS! Somehow, they must be controlling the kids and making them act like Bullies! Of course. When I walked up to the big kid this morning, the Shadow went away and the kid stopped teasing Aidan. So what do I do now? That Shadow's back and it brought all of it's friends. Maybe if I can get the Shadow off of Aidan first, he'll hear what the bullies are saying and know they are teasing him. But then what? There are like ten other Shadows. What will happen if they cling to me, or worst of all attack Aidan? I can't take that chance. I'm gonna need some help and I think I know just the person to ask.

When everyone rushes for the doors at lunch I stand outside the janitor's closet and wait. I see her coming and motion for her to follow me. I check to make sure no one is watching me and then slip inside the closet. A few seconds later, Rachel comes in and closes the door quickly behind her.

"What's going on? You know I'm not supposed to be seen with you, you're still being P.U.'d "

I reach behind her and lock the door.

"I know. That's what I want to talk to you about. I need you to get all the grade 6's together and come out to the swings and P.U. me."

She looks at me as if I've lost my mind.

"You want to be teased? What happened to keeping a low profile?"

"There is no time to explain." I whisper, "Please just bring them out, tell them whatever you need to."

For the first time since I met her, she doesn't know what to say, so I help her.

"Tell them I stink really bad today and get them to follow you. Once they're all teasing me, I need you to slip away and get the entire grade eights together. Now here is the hard part. Once you have the grade eights' attention, somehow you have to get them to come down to the swings as well."   She still stands there in front of me, blank.

"Please." I beg her, "You're the only friend I have."

Her eyes squint as if she doesn't believe me. She then nods, opens the door and walks out.

When I walk out onto the playground I see the bullies over by the swings, right where I knew they'd be. I take a deep breath and walk towards them. They pay no attention to me, because they are too busy teasing Aidan. As I get closer I look around, but I don't see Rachel anywhere. The Shadows on the bullies' backs see me coming and their eyes begin to glow. Come on, where are you Rachel? I can't believe she just blew me off! I'm on my own. Some friend. Who needs her? Just as I reach the swings I hear someone yell behind me.

"There he is. Doesn't he know how to take a bath?"

I turn around. It's Rachel! She's walking towards me, followed by my entire grade six class. Rachel plugs her nose and keeps saying how stinky I am, but the other grade six's aren't joining in. Why? I look back at Aidan and the bullies. Right, the grade six's aren't naturally mean, they have no Shadow bullies controlling them. Well, I guess if they don't have their own bullies, I'll have to do the job for them.

I look back at Rachel and yell, "The wind is blowing that way, so you must be smelling all your own stink!"

I turn and see one of the Shadows on Aidan's bullies look over. I hear one of the grade six's behind me say,

"That's not very nice. I don't stink…you stink."

Suddenly the Shadow let's go of the little kid's back and flies over, attaching itself to the grade six that yelled at me. The grade six starts teasing me hard, but it's not enough, the Shadow covering Aidan's ears still hangs on. I wink at Rachel and she joins in the teasing. They both start flinging insults at me and all of a sudden I feel something cold cover my ears. That's it! I look at Aidan and as the other kids tease him, his face turns red with embarrassment. I can't hear what they are saying, but it must be really mean, because Aidan looks like he is about to cry.

I yell to him "Don't let them see it bothers you! Ignore them!"

Aidan looks at me scared.

"It's gonna be okay."

I pull my binoculars out of my backpack and toss them to Aidan. "Look at their backs!" I tell him.

Aidan puts the binoculars to his eyes and his face goes white.

"Pashawn!" he gasps.

"You see them now. Ignore them!"

Aidan turns and walks away, but the bullies follow him. The grade six bully keeps teasing me and I nod at Rachel. It's time for plan B. As she slips away I call over to Aidan.

"When I tell you to, I need you to bark."

He looks at me confused.

"Trust me." I tell him.

Off in the distance by the thick line of trees, I see Rachel coming with the grade eights. They are all well into puberty and are as tall as some of the teachers. I yell to Aidan "Bark!"

Aidan, still confused, starts to bark.

"More." I yell and he barks louder.

Soon his bullies are all barking back, teasing him. When the grade eights get within hearing distance I yell to Aidan "Stop!" He does, but his bullies keep on barking loudly.

The grade eights stare at the bullies, barking and acting crazy. It's working!

I yell over to Aidan, "See, the best thing to do with a bully is ignore them, but sometimes you need to give a bully a taste of it's own medicine!"

Like I planned, the grade eights burst out laughing. As they point and laugh at the bullies, the Shadows on their backs begin to shake. They don't like this at all. I point at the bullies and laugh. Soon the entire grade six's have joined in too. The Shadows shake so fast they become just a blur of grey and then are swallowed up in flames and disappear into a puff of smoke. Suddenly I can hear again. The Shadow covering my ears must have gone too. I walk over to Aidan and give him a hug, he holds on extra tight. Soon the laughing stops and all the kids walk away, no longer interested. I let go of Aidan and he walks over to play in the sandbox with a group of grade three's. That's how it is in grade school, one moment something can seem like it's the end of the world and the next moment, everyone has forgotten about it, even you. I watch him play with the other little kids for a little bit, no Shadows, just giggling and happiness. And there it is, his smile has come back! Somewhere deep inside, my best friend still exists. Someday soon I hope we can talk about all this, in real words, but for now, that smile will do.

I head back towards the school and as I reach the front steps, Rachel pops her head out around the corner. I know we aren't supposed to be seen talking to each other, but I have to thank her. This plan would have never worked without her. I look around and make sure no one is looking and then whisper, "Thank you."

She looks around too and then replies "Woof."

(the eighth scroll)

A few years ago my family went on a road trip. Like always, Mama and Dad didn't tell us where we were going. They said that if we knew, we'd be thinking about how long it takes to get there, instead of enjoying the ride. Aidan and I had the back seat all set up with everything we needed for the journey; DVD player, video games, books, paper and pencil crayons, pillows, blankets, MP3 players and snacks. Old Rusty may look a little rough, but her back seat is huge. There is enough room for Aidan and I to both lie down and sleep. I used to love long road trips, the smell of Old Rusty's leather seats and summer air, Mama and Dad quietly talking in the front, the soft sound of the radio playing, looking out the window at the old farm houses and wondering who lives there. Sometimes I would just turn off my games and close my eyes and take it all in. At night, the car was lit up by the lights on the dashboard and Dad would roll up all the windows. The only sounds would be the hum of the engine, the radio and the soft rumble of Mama snoring as we winded down the road. I had some of my best sleeps in the back of that car, but this wasn't one of them. My head started to flop from side to side, bouncing off my pillow that was pressed against the door. I opened my eyes and looked out the front window. The fog was so thick and it was so dark, I couldn't see past the headlights. I wasn't the only one; Dad was gripping the steering wheel so tight that his knuckles were white and he was swearing under his breath. I looked over to see if Aidan was still sleeping, but he wasn't, he was hunched over his video game, with his headphones on. You'd think I'd be happy that he was unaware of the dangerous road we were driving on, except for one thing; Aidan gets carsick. It's not his fault, Mama gets carsick too, so he must have inherited it from her. Normally he is okay, as long as he isn't looking down, has a clear view of the road and the window is open. I leaned forward and said to Dad " Aidan's playing video games. Maybe he should stop." My Dad just kept his eyes on the road and said, " Not now Cailum, this road is horrible and I can't see four flipping feet in front of this car!" Mama knows how bad carsickness is, but my Dad believes that it's all in their heads. Just then, Aidan raised his head and dropped his video game onto his lap. He moaned. I reached over and pulled his earphones out for him." Just look out the front window." I told him. Aidan leaned forward, but I guess the fog was so thick, that the view didn't help. I said, " Open your window." Aidan tried the button, but it didn't work. Dad had the child locks on. Aidan's face went white and I yelled to Dad " Open Aidan's window Dad." My Dad shouted back," It's freezing outside, if we open the window the heater has to work harder and the car will suck more gas." " What's going on?" My Mama asked. She must have been woken up by all the yelling." Aidan is gonna blow!" I screamed." Open his window!" Mama yelled. " It's locked!" I told her. Aidan covered his mouth." Open the window!" Mama yelled at Dad. " Can't you see I'm driving!" he replied. " Aidan is gonna be sick!" she said and reached over Dad to unlock the windows. As she reached over, she knocked Dad's hand and the car swerved." Stop it!" Dad yelled, " You'll kill us all!" Aidan leaned forward and tapped Dad on the shoulder. Dad looked in the rear view mirror and said, " Just look out the window. It's all in your head. Mind over matter Aidan, just think, I'm not sick...say it with me." Aidan just shook his head no." Just stop the car." Mama said. " No." yelled Dad, " This fog is so thick that if anyone is behind us, they'll smash right into us." He tried using a calm voice " Just say I'm not sick." Aidan shook his head again. Dad ordered, " Say it....say it!" Aidan took his hand away from his mouth, " I'M NOT SICK!" he yelled and just as my Dad said, " See I told you..." A fountain of barf flew out of Aidan's mouth, covering Dad and splashing onto the windshield. Dad slammed on the brakes and pulled the car over. Aidan and I sat back and waited for Dad to lose it. Everything went silent. Dad just sat there, covered in barf. Mama's eyes darted back and forth between Dad and us. Then I heard a noise. BZZZZZZ! Aidan's window rolled down. Dad said calmly, still facing forward " I said say it...not spray it!" He took off his shirt and wiped the inside of the windshield then he opened his door and got out. The three of us watched Dad walk in front of the car. His body was steaming from the hot puke in the cold night air. Mama started to giggle. He then took off his pants and was left standing in only his socks and shoes and white underwear. He went to throw his clothes into the bushes, but couldn't see the ditch because of the fog and fell down into it. When he stood up his underpants had fallen around his ankles. He bent over to pull them up and right then a truck drove by, honking it's horn. Someone yelled from the truck "FULL MOON!" and Aidan and I started to laugh. Dad quickly pulled up his underwear and Aidan and I stopped laughing as he got back into the car. My Mama said, "That was the only pair of pants you brought. Should we just go home?" My Dad growled, "Nope." He started the car and drove the rest of the way in his underwear. When we got to our surprise destination, my Dad had to wrap one of the car's floor mats around himself inside. The hello hugs were awkward and although my Dad hates to be wrong, he finally accepted the pink pair of sweatpants my Aunt offered him.

It's warm today and Old Rusty has that familiar smell of leather and summer. Underneath it, I can still smell a little puke and I remember Dad in his underwear.

I sniff and say, "Full Moon!" to Aidan and we both laugh.

I'm glad Mama picked us up from school, because after dealing with the bullies, I just don't have the energy to run up the driveway. When we get to the house, I drag myself inside and flop on the couch in the front room. I think Mama asked me if I want a snack, but before I know it, I'm dreaming.

Dad is in his underwear, riding a bull with his socks and shoes on and wearing earmuffs. My eyes pop open. I look around the room and the orange afternoon sunlight is shining through the windows. I try to sit up, but I can't move. I try again but I'm stuck. Oh no, it's happening again. Sleep Paralysis. I can't speak or move, but I can see. I remember what the doctor told me and I try to relax. Relax. What was that? Over by the curtains I see something move. It's not a Shadow, more like a mist. I feel it getting closer. Am I imagining this? I close my eyes and try harder to let go, because the doctor said fighting it will only make it worse. I try to take a couple of deep breaths, but suddenly it's hard to breathe. It feels like something heavy is sitting on my chest and all I can do is take tiny, quick breaths. I open my eyes and sitting on my chest is a thick, grey mist. I struggle to get it off. I try my hardest to scream, but I can't and

112

the mist just keeps getting heavier. I shut my eyes tight and say over and over in my head, "Go away. Go away!"

I hear a loud cackle.

I squeeze my eyes tighter. The cackle gets louder and it feels like something is trying to open my eyes, so I force them closed. Cold, long fingernails pry my eyelids open. Light starts to come in and I see a bony, old woman with matted red hair and long nose, leaning over me. The Old Hag! Mama said that's what they called it. This must be her! Her cold, rough hand holds my head still. She raises her other hand and her green, cracked nails get longer. She looks down at my chest and cackles again. I try to move with everything I have, but I still can't. She thrusts her pointed nails down towards my chest. I close my eyes and wait for her nails to dig into me. I feel my legs kick, up and down. I can move! I open my eyes and the Old Hag is gone. I jump up off of the couch, run into the kitchen where Mama is. I know that besides the tree, this is the safest place to be and so I stick to her like glue until bedtime.

The alarm clock hits 3 a.m. and I'm still sitting here, on the top bunk, wide-awake, while Aidan sleeps soundly beside me. There is no way I can sleep after what happened. I've had Sleep Paralysis before and felt something in the room. I've even had trouble breathing, but I've never had a witch sitting on my chest. She wasn't just chill'n out, The Old Hag was gonna stick those long nails into me. So far so good though, I'm still awake and I haven't seen or heard her. Shadows still wisp around on the floor, but no witch. As I look down at the Shadows flying across the floor, I notice something in the corner. Is it the Hag? I reach over Aidan, grab the flashlight and point it at the corner. I click the switch and realize it's just a pile of Aidan's clothes. As usual he didn't throw them in the hamper. I shine the flashlight around the room, just to make sure there are no other surprises hiding in the corners and I notice something strange. As my light shines around the room, the Shadows move away from the light. Over and over I try to shine the light on the Shadows and every time they move out of the way.

"You got to be kidding me. All this time, I've been chased by Shadows and all we had to do to keep them away was shine a flashlight at them?"

Finally, I corner one of the Shadows between the wall and the toy box. There is nowhere for it to escape. I take my aim, shine the light directly at it and in a puff of smoke, it disappears! No wonder they're so afraid of the light.

"This is better than video games!"

For a while I hang over the edge of the bed and shoot at the Shadows, clicking the flashlight off and on like a laser gun and every time the light hits them they disappear.

About an hour later, all this excitement has reached my bladder and I need to use the washroom. Although shooting the Shadows from the top bunk is fun, after turning a few of their buddies into puffs of smoke, I'm sure they'd like to return the favor. But as worried as I am, my bladder waits for no one, so I grab my flashlight and climb down the vine ladder to the floor. Clearing a path through the darkness with my flashlight, I make it to the bathroom and turn on the light. I take my time, read a few of Mama's gossip magazines, play toilet paper basketball, even brush my teeth again, cause it's not like I've got anywhere else I have to be. When I finished correcting the word searches in all of Mama's magazines, I decide I should probably go back and make sure Aidan is okay.

Again, I clear a path in front of me with my flashlight, but as I reach the middle of the hall, I realize that I left it on the whole time I was in the bathroom. It starts to flicker and I start to walk faster. A few steps away from our bedroom door, my worst fear happens...the flashlight goes out! I press the button on the flashlight, but nothing happens. I press it again. Nothing. I bang it against my hand and still no light. The hallway is pitch black, but I can see the moonlight coming through our bedroom window, so I start to run for it. Behind me I hear the floor creaking. I look back and see Shadows coming out of the walls, the ceiling and the floor and they look angry! Suddenly, they form into one giant Shadow and start chasing after me. I run as hard as I can and when I reach our room I dive across the floor, roll towards the vine ladder, jump up onto it and land on the third step. I climb up as fast as I can and don't look down until I reach the top. At the bottom of the vine ladder, the giant Shadow stands staring up at me. It then circles the ladder a few times, but doesn't try to come up. After a minute or two, it breaks apart into smaller Shadows and they fly off out of our room. I crawl to the other side of the bed where we keep the flashlights. I grab the silver one and flick the switch, but it's batteries are out of juice too. I bang it against the side of the bed but still no luck. Great, now I'm stuck up here until morning. Why doesn't anyone buy batteries? Angry, I chuck the flashlight across the bed and it hits the railing hard. The flashlight turns on. Awesome, I can play Shadow laser again! I crawl over to grab it and notice there's something scratched into the railing...words.

Shadows far,
Shadows near,
Doesn't matter cause,
I'm safe up here.
All night long,
They'll leave me be,
Cause they don't like this bed,
That's made of tree.
M.K.

M.K.? Who's M.K.? M.K….M.K...Marty Kokotilo? He wrote this? He saw Shadows too! No matter what, I'm safe up here…bed made of tree! That must be why the Shadows stopped at the bottom of the ladder and don't come up here. The bunk bed must be made of some kind of special wood. Then, I remember how the Shadow in the greenhouse wouldn't come near the big tree. This bed must be made of the same wood. Yes of course, even the Old Hag hasn't bugged me tonight because I'm up here. This afternoon I fell asleep on the couch down stairs, not on the bunk bed. I'm safe up here. We're safe. I look around and somehow I feel like Marty is watching me.

"Thank you Marty."

I crawl back beside Aidan, climb under the covers and lay down, no longer worrying about the Shadows that swirl below.

"We're safe." I whisper as I wrap my arm around Aidan. I close my eyes and I see Dad in his underwear again, only this time he's dancing. I laugh, because he's a horrible dancer. He spins around and around until his underwear falls down.

"Full Moon!" I yell and that's when I realize I'm dreaming.

to et se

(the ninth scroll)

Dad and I worked on the old fort every weekend for two months. One Saturday, I got up extra early because we needed to get an early start on the roof. The weekend before we had finally got the walls up and I couldn't wait to see it all put together. When I came downstairs, Dad was already eating breakfast. "I was thinking the same thing. That roof is going to take us a while so it's best we start early." I said. My Dad got up and that's when I noticed he wasn't wearing his work clothes. He was wearing a suit and tie. "A little dressed up for the fort aren't you?" I asked. "Not today, son." He said. "I have to go to work. There is a new housing development over on High Street and I'm meeting with the builders to see if I can get the drywall contract." I looked at him angry" It's the weekend. You work all week. Everyday. The weekend is supposed to be ours. We have to do the roof! Can't you meet them on Monday?" My Dad said nothing and just rinsed his cereal bowl in the sink. "Come on, Dad. You promised." I told him. He turned to me. "Well, things come up. That's life. Next weekend, alright?" I got really angry," I hate your stupid job!" My Dad grabbed me by the shoulder and said," Look at me. If I don't work, we don't eat. You don't understand right now but when you're older you will. It's just a fort Cailum, it can wait!" I pulled away from him, ran out the kitchen door and took off down the street. Even when I heard Mama calling me back, I just kept running.

I spent the rest of the day by the creek, skipping stones, catching minnows and crawfish, and laying in the sun. Around dinner time my stomach started to hurt. I hadn't eaten all day and as mad as I was with my Dad, I still needed to eat. I thought about trying to eat the crawfish, but I didn't like the thought of killing them, so I let them go. I walked back to my house and when I got there, I saw Old Rusty wasn't in the driveway, so I knew my Dad wasn't home yet. I thought I'd go in, eat whatever Mama made for dinner and go straight up to my room. That way I wouldn't have to see Dad.

I went into the kitchen and turned on the lights. There was a sandwich sitting on the table. I scarfed it down and pounded the glass of water that was beside it. As I took my last gulp, I heard banging coming from outside. I got up and walked out the kitchen door. The banging got louder! I went around the corner to the side of the house and saw the most incredible thing. There was a roof on our fort! Dad! I knew he wouldn't let me down. He must have come back and worked nonstop to build it. "Dad!" I yelled. "Yeah?" Dad said behind me. I turned around and hugged him. "I'm so sorry I was such a jerk." Dad rubbed my head, "No son, it was me who was the jerk. I'm sorry." I turned back and looked at the new roof, "It's amazing!" I said. "Sure is." he replied. I looked up and sitting on the peak of the roof was Mama. "Not bad, huh?" she asked. "It's awesome!" I said, "But you should probably get down from there Mama, you could hurt yourself." Mama looked at me and smiled "In a minute, I just have a few more nails to put in!" I turned to Dad "Oh, I get it, she helped you right?" He shook his head, "No. I just got home." Mama called out from the top of the roof. "Your Dad's not the only one that can swing a hammer." It wasn't just any old roof. It had rounded sides so that the wind couldn't get under it. A high pitch so that the rain would roll off it and heat coils between the shingles and the wood, so the snow would melt off of it. It was the strongest part of the fort and my Mama built it.

T.G.I.S. "Thank goodness it's Saturday!" After finding what Marty scratched into the railing, I've decided that Aidan and I should turn the bunk bed into a fort. Marty said the Shadows were scared of the wood the bunk beds are made of, but what if the monsters I've seen at school show up here? They may not be as afraid of the wood as the Shadows, so I figure we need to be prepared.

Apparently, pencils are in short supply around our house, because the only thing I can find to draw plans for our fort with is a purple crayon. It's hard to make a professional looking blue print in purple crayon, but I sit on the floor of our room, drawing up the plans for our "Purple Wood Fort." I think I may have been all wrong about Uncle Marty. He scratched that message into the wood so someone would find it and if he wanted someone to find it, was it so he could help them? Maybe he's on our side. Yeah, it can't be the ghost of Marty that's haunting us, because we are being chased by a bunch of Shadows, not a just one Shadow. Also, the message he left said he was being scared by Shadows too. Maybe he isn't dead. Maybe the Shadows scared him so bad that he ran away? He could have gone to stay with an Aunt or an Uncle. Mama never told us she had a brother, so who knows what other relatives there are that we don't know about. Wherever he is, he's probably happy because he isn't being haunted anymore.

As I struggle to draw the fort with the little nub of the crayon, Aidan walks in holding a sheet of paper.

"Sashawn" he says and holds the paper up in front of his face.

Now I know why this crayon is so little, he must have used most of it to draw his own plans for the fort. He was too little to help Dad and I build our own fort, but he must have been watching because the plans he's drawn are amazing. They may be purple but they have just the right amount of everything; tech, camouflage and defense. I know he is struggling with his words still, but man is he smart. As I look over his drawings I realize that we are going to need a butt load of supplies, which means we aren't going to be able to keep this a secret from Mama. With all the noise we'll be making and the supplies we'll be scrounging from around the house, we're gonna have to tell her something.

We sit down to breakfast, our usual Saturday special; pancakes, bacon and eggs. Aidan and I are gonna need to get going on the fort right after breakfast, so I better talk to her now. I think the best angle is to play the sympathy card.

"Mama, we really miss our tree fort." I say, testing to see her reaction.

She turns to me with a concerned look on her face so I press on.

"...and we've been thinking that we need a new place that's just boys only, like our fort used to be."

She loves it when we're playing "nice" together and without me saying another word she smiles and says, "Sure."

Wow, that was easy. I had a whole speech planned with reasons to every "no" she could possibly give. I even had backups to my backups, but I know when to stop talking so I just say, "Great. Thank you Mama."

Aidan and I shovel our food into our mouths as fast as we can, but before we can finish, Mama asks "Are you guys going to build in the gardens or out back?"

I knew this was too easy. I try to avoid the question.

"Well actually..."

She jumps in .

"I can help. Dad's not the only..."

I cut her off. "...one that can swing a hammer, I know. Mama, we really need to do this on our own..."

I see her face turn sad and I catch myself.

"Aidan didn't get to build the last one and you always say that too many cooks in the kitchen..."

She sighs, "Spoil the soup."

As I prepared, first I use one of her own sayings against her, then I flatter her.

"You're such a great builder..." I say. "...and we're

afraid that if you help, we'll just get lazy and let you do all the work."

She blushes "That's okay. I like to build."

I shake my head "No, no, no. We should do this on our own. But if you let us get a dog, you could help us build the dog house."

I know I'm going a little too far, but if you never ask, you'll never know. She gives me a disapproving look.

"Now you're pushing it. I get it. Just build your fort."

We run out of the kitchen, not wanting to leave room for a word more. As we reach the stairs I yell back "By the way, we're gonna build it in our room."

Before she can answer we race up the stairs and close our bedroom door.

A few seconds later there's a knock at the door. Aidan and I open the door a crack and poke our heads out.

"Yes?"

"Pashawn?"

Mama stands there, unimpressed.

"Boys, you are not building a fort in your bedroom."

Now it's time for the begging.

"But Mama, those gardens are really scary and it's not like we're building a real fort, just hanging some sheets and cardboard and stuff."

Mama looks suspicious "Just sheets and cardboard?"

"And stuff." I answer.

"Ooookay" she says, still suspicious and tries to push open the door.

I quickly hold up a sign we made that says "No Girls" and hang it on the doorknob.

"No girls?" Mama asks.

"It's kinda part of our boys only thing."

"Fine." she says, "But don't wreck anything."

I nod my head and quickly close the door. I hate lying to Mama, but if I tell her everything, the Shadows, or worse may start picking on her and I can't take that chance. All she needs to know is that we are building a fort.

For the next seven days we kept out of Mama's way. We hung the "No Girls" sign on the door and even tucked ourselves in at night to avoid her seeing our fortress. We woke up before she did and only used the power tools when she was cleaning. With the sound of the vacuum and her heavy metal music blaring, she can't hear anything. For a solid week we worked every night after school and by the next weekend every piece of Aidan's plan was completed. We've pushed the heavy dresser against the closet and put three chairs on top of it, to form a barricade. Under the bed, we've stuffed empty moving boxes and filled in any space left around them with clothes. Nothing gonna get under there now. Every flashlight and glow stick we could find has been hung from the ceiling so it is never fully dark in here. I invented and installed a reverse periscope that runs from the top bunk to the floor, so we can check for Shadows without having to look over the edge of the bed. In the hall, we hid the camera from an old cell phone and the microphone from one of Aidan's toys, high up on the wall. We attached them both to an old T.V. and stereo unit, up on the top bunk. This will come in really handy when we have to make a trip to the bathroom at night or need a "heads up" when Mama's coming. We took off the vine ladder and made a ramp up to the second bunk using an old door. I attached a rope and pulley to it so we can raise and lower it like a drawbridge. Now when we're on the top bunk, there's no way for the monsters to get up here. We reinforced the bedroom door with a bunch of bars and locks that I can also control from the top bunk using another pulley system. To hide this all from Mama, we hung sheets off the sides, stapled a cardboard roof on and put up the pair of "Old Man Cummings" underpants I brought from our old fort. Now it looks just like the kinda fort a kid makes to watch cartoons from on Saturday morning. Dad always said "If you're in hot water with a girl, you can distract her with compliments", so as an added touch, we wrote the words "Mama's roof" on the cardboard roof to make her feel good.

Even though we now have the fort finished, the Shadows haven't gone away. If anything they've gotten louder and there is more of them than ever before. Since we barricaded the closet and filled in the space under the bed, they've started to squeeze through any crack they can find. They're not really scaring us anymore; in fact, it's like they're watching us, checking in every night to see what else we have added to the fort. Whatever they're doing, two great things have happened because of this fort. One: I'm starting to feel a bit better. Keeping busy and doing something about what was bothering us, instead of just worrying about it, has made the days pass by and helped me feel not so helpless. Two: With our fort protecting us now, and the days are flying by, we've made it through the twelve sleeps. That's two weeks. That means today's the day we get to go to Dad's new place for the whole weekend! I don't know what I'm more excited about, seeing Dad, or Aidan and I being as far away from these Shadows as possible and maybe getting a full nights sleep.

Before the sun even came up this morning, Aidan and I have been busy getting ready to see Dad. We both took a bath, without Mama asking. I combed my hair and put on some cologne; Aidan washed his puppy P.J.'s and put on one of Dad's old ties on over top of them. I got into my very best clothes and we both brushed our teeth. Twice! I made Aidan and

I breakfast and even brought some up for Mama, so she could have breakfast in bed. It's been two weeks since they've seen each other and we want her to be in a good mood. When she finished her breakfast, Aidan went into her closet and picked out a fancy red dress for her to wear. Mama said it was a little "too much" for seven o'clock in the morning, so she went with the pink tracksuit instead.

I drop the last of our ten bags off at the front door and look over them to make sure we have absolutely everything. Aidan is sitting on top of the pile, keeping watch for any sign of Dad. Mama walks up just as I see that we forgot our sleeping bags.

"Wow. Where are you going?" she asks.

"To get our sleeping bags." I say and run past her.

"Are you sure you don't want to bring your fort?"

"You know I thought about it, but it's not really portable."

I turn to go up the stairs, but the look on her face tells me she wasn't being serious.

"Park it! This is way too much stuff. Unless your father is driving a moving truck, you only need one bag."

She looks around at the mountain of bags.

"It's only one weekend, sweetie. Take all this back upstairs and just put a few clothes into a small bag, that's all you need."

I whistle for Aidan and he climbs down off the mountain of luggage. I load him up like pack horse and we drag our bags back up to our room. When we get there I drop everything on the floor and start rooting through them, trying to pick out the important things. I'm having a hard time deciding what to bring. Dad never told us where we were going or what we were doing and I want to be prepared. I begin to panic, Dad is supposed to be here any minute. I start stuffing a little bag full of everything that's within my reach. I think I put in a toque, an eraser, one left shoe, maybe a right one, a candle...I'm not even sure if I put underwear in there...BING! BONG! The old doorbell is so loud it sounds more like a church bell than a doorbell, but I know what it means. "Dad's here!"

Before Mama can even call us, Aidan and I shut our bedroom door and are running down the hall. I get to the top of the stairs and I see Dad standing at the front door. It's crazy, I know, but even though it's only been two weeks, I was starting to forget what he looks like. Sometimes when I'm afraid at night, I try hard to picture him, standing in our room, protecting us. But looking at him standing there at the front door, my heart starts beating fast and I feel like I'm gonna cry. I run down the stairs and jump into his arms. He's big and strong and he wraps me in his arms so tight I can barely breathe. But I don't care. Thud! I feel Aidan slam against me and now he's holding both of us in his arms, high off the ground, just like the day we left.

Aidan kisses Dad all over his face. It's kinda his thing. Dad knows the drill and lets him go to it. First the chin, then mouth and cheeks, then the eyes, the forehead and finally, he takes a deep whiff of his hair and kisses the top of his head. Mama just stands to the side forcing a half smile. I'm sure all this attention on Dad is bothering her. I tap Dad on the shoulder and he lets me go. I grab Mama around the waist and hug her tight. I think it's just what she needed, because she hugs me back twice as tight.

"All aboard." Dad says and starts to walk out the door, "The ship's leaving."

Aidan drops down out of Dad's arms and gives Mama the whole kiss routine.

I yell, "Aye aye Captain" and grab our bag.

When Aidan and I walk outside, there's Dad standing beside a shiny new car. It's a red convertible!

"You like it?" he asks.

Aidan yells "Pashawn" but Mama doesn't look too impressed.

Dad looks at her then says, "Aw relax, it's a rental."

Mama still doesn't look impressed.

"It's all they had." Dad says.

"Uh, huh." Mama groans.

I know where this is going, so I open the passenger door, climb in and honk the horn.

"Okay" Dad's tone changes, "All aboard! Time to hit the road."

Aidan opens the door and I lean forward so he can climb into the tiny back seat. I wave to Mama standing on the porch.

"I love you." She says, "See you in two days."

Dad starts up the car and as it starts to move it jerks a little.

"Sticky clutch." Dad says and then the wheels screech and we take off like a rocket down the driveway.

The speed of the car moving forward pushes my body into the seat. I can't turn my head but I can see Mama in the side mirror. Even though we are pretty far down the road, I can tell that now she's really, really, really not impressed.

tọ etọ et šɛ

(the tenth scroll)

Mama and Dad started to go to marriage counselling on Saturday mornings, downtown. Dad didn't really want to go and said," It was a waste of money", but Mama insisted. Dad finally caved but said he didn't want to pay for a babysitter, so we had to go with them. While they took turns going in to see the counsellor, we waited at an old diner across the street that my Dad called " a greasy spoon" and ate lunch.

One Saturday, Aidan had his first " club house" sandwich. It was huge. Three stories of meat, cheese, lettuce, tomato, mayo and bacon, all held together with a long toothpick that had a frilly plastic thing on the end. Dad came back from the counsellor and wouldn't say anything. He just sat down and motioned for Mama to go for her turn. It must have been a really rough session that day, because my Dad wouldn't even look at Mama. Now, I'm always hungry, but when I get nervous or worried, I turn into a pig, so as I watched Mama leave, I stuffed my face full of french toast and sausages. Aidan is the opposite. Normally he isn't much of a big eater, but when he's nervous he completely loses his appetite. So after eating only a few bites, he pushed his plate to the side. That's when he started to get bored. Normally we brought our video games with us, but that day we were in such a rush that we forgot them at home. Aidan started tapping the knife on the table, but Dad took his knife away. He played with the salt and peppershakers, making them fight till the death, until Dad took them away too. He turned the napkin holder on its side and made his fingers bounce on it like it was a trampoline, but Dad grabbed that and gave it back to the waitress. Aidan didn't understand. He just wanted my Dad's attention, but my Dad just wasn't in the mood. Aidan tried talking to him, but Dad couldn't deal with Aidan's new made up language and kept saying " Not now." No matter how hard Aidan tried, my Dad just kept staring out the window. After a while I thought Aidan may have gotten the point, but then it happened.

I looked over and saw Aidan slowly take the toothpick out of one half of his club house sandwich. He then pulled the straw out of his milk glass gently, watching Dad the whole time, making sure to not get caught. I thought he was just trying to play with something quietly and didn't want Dad to see, because he'd take it away from him. But then I saw a twinkle in his eye and I realized that he had a plan. I shook my head, "No" but he just kept going. He put the toothpick into the straw, slowly raised it to his mouth and filled his cheeks with air. Just then my Mama snuck up behind us and said "Boo!" It scared the heck out of Aidan and he lost control of his lips, releasing the air in his mouth and shooting the toothpick out of the straw, like blow dart. At the exact same moment, Dad turned to look and the toothpick hit him in the face, just missing his eye! The toothpick hit his face so hard; the tip of it broke off, and got stuck inside his cheek!

Although it was an accident, I think my Dad believes Aidan was actually trying to blind him, because now anytime Aidan wants my Dad's attention, he just points to his eye and my Dad drops whatever he's doing and listens.

Dad kept both eyes on Aidan, who was working up a sweat, showing him his new dance moves. I don't know if you can really call it dancing, because it mostly consists of him thrusting his hips. While Dad was laughing at how inappropriate Aidan's hip thrusts are, I looked around the new apartment. It only has two bedrooms and one bathroom, but it's new, not old, dusty and haunted like Mama's house. He made up one of the bedrooms for Aidan and I and hung some of our artwork in it. There is only one bed in it, but it's no big deal, because Aidan and I have been sleeping in the same bed for two weeks now. Well, maybe not sleeping, but it's still okay. Beside the bed is a little table with a flashlight on it. Thank goodness, because in all the rush of repacking I forgot to pack ours. I know there are no Shadows here, but it still makes me feel better. Behind the flashlight is a picture of all three of us, buried under a pile of leaves from our old backyard. It's a great picture, but something, actually someone very important, is missing from it. I know that I will see Mama tomorrow, but I already miss her and being here, seeing that picture, reminds me that we aren't a family anymore.

As I stand staring at the picture, wondering if Mama's okay, I hear Aidan yell.

"Pashawn".

I run to the living room to see what's wrong, but they aren't there. I check the kitchen, then the bathroom, but I can't find them. Where are they? Did the Shadows follow us? Did they take them? I start to panic.

"Out here."

I turn around and I'm relieved to see Dad and Aidan on the balcony. Aidan is jumping up and down so much that Dad has to hold him still so he won't fall over the railing.

"A little help." Dad shouts.

I walk out to see what Aidan is so worked up about and Dad points down over the railing.

"Surprise!"

I look over the railing and down below is a huge, outdoor swimming pool, with crystal clear water, a slide and two diving boards just begging to be jumped off of. Suddenly I'm panicked again; in all the packing and unpacking I didn't stuff any swim shorts into our bag. Great, there is an amazing water playground right below us and we have nothing to wear.

I look at Dad, "We didn't bring bathing suits."

Dad stares at me for a second, I guess he realizes that he should of given us a heads up. Just when I think all we are gonna be able to do with the pool is stare at it, he shrugs his shoulders and says,

"No worries. You guys can just wear a pair of my shorts."

I think Mama must be the one who buys all of our clothing, because Dad clearly has no idea what size we are.

As I expected, the shorts are huge. Aidan and I each pull on a pair of his enormous shorts and walk out into the living room, holding them up with both hands. Dad looks us up and down.

"A little big, huh? Wait right here."

He runs off to his bedroom and comes back holding bungee cords in each of his hands.

"Ta-Da!" he says proudly.

"What are we gonna do with bungee cords?" I ask

Dad shakes his head.

"Bungee cords? Nooooo, these aren't bungee cords. They're stretchy...hooking... swim short belts!"

Before I can say no, he's wrapping one around my waist. Although it looks silly, it actually works. He tries to wrap one around Aidan's waist but it's too small, so Dad runs back to his room and comes out holding another bungee. He hooks one end of each bungee to the front of Aidan's shorts and the other end of each to the back.

He claps his hands together "Stretchy, hooking...swim short suspenders!"

After a couple of minutes, Aidan and I didn't care what we were wearing, because we were having so much fun! We spent the rest of the day in our giant shorts and bungee cords, swimming and playing with Dad. I don't know what has gotten into him, but he seems to have a lot more energy than he used too. He must have given Aidan and I, like twenty dolphin rides each and then played "Marco Polo" until we couldn't swim another stroke. It still sucks that Mama and Dad aren't together, but I have to admit Mama was right; they are better parents being apart. Dad laughs a lot more and now all his attention is on us.

As the sun went down, we had a barbeque by the pool and Dad made the greasiest, sloppiest, most delicious burgers ever. Normally I eat my burgers plain, but this time I ate two of them, with the works; lettuce, tomato, pickles, mustard, relish and ketchup. Later that night we watched a zombie movie that I know Mama would never allow us to watch. When the movie ended, I got up and started to walk towards the bedroom.

Dad asked, "Where are you going?"

I said, "It's bed time, isn't it?"

Dad scoffed and said, "Not unless you want it to be."

My mouth dropped and he said, "New house. New rules. From now on, you fall asleep when you're ready."

I "high-fived" Dad and hopped over the back of the couch.

"First zombies." Dad said, "Now drop kicks!" and he turned on an old Kung Fu movie.

I pulled the blanket over Aidan and I and then we curled up on either side of him to watch the butt-kicking awesomeness!

"AAAAAAAAHHHHHHH!!!!!!" Aidan screams and I sit straight up. I didn't realize I'd fallen asleep. I think we're in the room Dad made up for us. He must have carried us in here after the Kung Fu movie. Aidan keeps screaming while he covers his eyes. He's still wearing his mittens. I strain to see in the dark and as my eyes focus, a big, black Shadow steps out of the closet! I reach over and grab the flashlight from the side table and shine it into the closet, so the Shadow will disappear. The bright light cuts through the darkness of the closet like a knife. I sweep it across the hanging clothes and stop on the huge Shadow. It covers it's glowing yellow eyes and smoke rises from it's edges as it starts to fade. I hear a loud, deep laugh and then instead of disappearing into a puff of smoke, the Shadow gets bigger and bigger until it's so big it fills up half of the closet.

"What kind of batteries are in this flashlight?" I hear a deep, loud laugh again and just like the Shadows at school, it changes into a monster, but this time it doesn't change back.

It's color goes from black to green and as it moves towards us, it's footsteps are so heavy they make the floor shake. Yellow-green toenails dig into the wood floor, pulling it forward, knocking the clothes off their hangers. It's arms are so long, that it's wet knuckles drag on the ground and it's huge, lumpy head hangs out in front of it. Thick green goo, drips from it's mouth and nostrils as it breathes heavily in and out, sniffing the air, like it's trying to pick up our scent. Aidan starts to gag because the smell of rotting garbage coming from the monster is overwhelming. It turns it's lumpy head towards Aidan, open's it's large mouth and snaps at the air with it's rows of sharp, crooked teeth. The monster stops suddenly and snorts. It then tilts it's head to the side, as if it is trying to figure out who or what we are. After a second or two of studying us, the monster snaps it's head up and lets out a thunderous scream that's so loud, I have to plug my ears.

"DAAAAAAAAAAD!!!!!" I yell at the top of my lungs, even though I'm sure this monster's scream must have woken him up already. Before I can scream again, the light flicks on and Dad runs in to the room, swinging a golf club.

"Where is it?"

"Pashawn!" Aidan says and points at the closet.

Dad runs over to the closet and swings the golf club, but misses the monster. He raises the club high above his head and swings again, but the monster just steps to one side and snorts.

Over and over Dad pounds the hanging clothes in the closet yelling, "That will teach you to mess with my kids" and the monster keeps moving out of the way.

Suddenly Dad stops swinging the golf club and turns to us, huffing and puffing, trying to catch his breath.

"Got em'…nothing…to worry about. You can go back to

sleep."

"What are you doing?' I ask him. "The monster is still there."

My Dad turns around and looks into the closet.

"Where?"

I stand up on the bed and point, "Right there on the side."

The monster raises a tuff of hair on it's face, that I think is an eyebrow and twists it's giant mouth into an evil grin. Dad looks into the closet and then looks back at me.

"Don't you see him?" I ask and behind him I see the monster's evil smile get bigger. It shakes it's lumpy head "no" and Dad takes a couple more swings at the closet.

"I must have got him that time." Dad says and the monster starts to laugh, pointing at it's horrible yellow eyes and then at us.

I know what that means. It'll be watching. Dad stands in front of us, still catching his breath as the monster drags itself back into the closet and disappears in the darkness.

"How could you miss it? The monster was standing right there! It was a big, green, ugly thing." I yell.

"Oh yeah, I saw it" Dad says, but he's a horrible liar.

Dad closes the closet doors and whispers, "It must have been scared of me and ran away. I...uh...better put a magic... stool...in front of the door, so it won't come back."

Dad picks up a tiny footstool and puts it in front of the closet doors.

"That'll hold it." He says and claps his hands together. "So, with that taken care of, can we all go back to sleep?"

I snap back at him. "Are you blind? That stupid little stool won't protect us from anything."

By the look on his face, Dad is done pretending.

"Don't be smart with me." He says sternly and I just look down at the ground.

He walks over to the bed and sits down. I'm so mad I don't say a word and he just sighs.

"Listen." he says softly, "Whatever you saw wasn't real. Okay? I know it seems real, but it's just your imagination. But no matter what is going on, real or imagined, it's never okay to disrespect me."

"I'm sorry." I say back and he hugs me.

I pull back a little, look into his eyes and reason with him. "Okay, I get it. You think it's make believe. But, if it was only my imagination, then how did Aidan and I both imagine the same thing, at the exact same time?"

Dad just shakes his head.

"You probably just got each other all worked up. I looked and there was nothing in the closet."

I turn away from him, but he puts his hand on my shoulder

turning me back.

"Come on Cailum, aren't you getting a little old for monsters in the closet? Aidan's only eight so I understand, but you're almost twelve. It's time you grew out of this kind of stuff."

I pull away from him, angry.

He speaks softly again. "I think this is about more than a monster. This divorce has been hard on all of us. I'm scared too. But we need to work together, not against each other to get through it. Okay?"

Aidan hops across the bed and hugs him. I'm really mad at him, but I haven't seen him in two weeks and I don't want to spend what little time we have being angry, so I turn and hug him too.

"Hey, I have an idea." He says, "Why don't the two of you climb into my bed."

I look up at him disappointed, "You don't get it, do you? A snuggle isn't gonna..."

Dad stops me. "Maybe not, but my room doesn't have a closet."

Aidan and I look at each other.

"No closet, means no green monsters..." I say and before I can finish, Aidan takes off down the hall.

I call right side." I yell and jump out of the bed and chase after him. As I dive into Dad's big bed he shouts, "Make sure to leave some room for me. I'll be there in a minute."

Aidan and I bury ourselves into Dad's heavy blankets and I see a light turn on in the hall. I can hear the beeps of a phone dialing and then Dad speaking quietly.

"Sashawn?" Aidan asks.

"Sshh!" I hush Aidan and sit up in the bed, trying to listen to what he's saying.

"I know it's late...that's why I called...they're freaked out...Aidan was screaming and Cailum keeps saying that there is something in the closet...Nicole...Nicole...are you there? What do you mean, we are too old?...slow down...Emaji-Nation. I know, it's all in their imagination...What's that?...You're starting to sound like the kids...Call who?...No you don't need to call anyone...She's crazy, you told me yourself...No way...I told you, I don't believe in all that mumbo jumbo!...I'm sorry I yelled...I just called to see if you had any ideas on how I can calm them down...you're better at this stuff than I am...Yeah, they're in my bed now. Okay, okay...I won't let them out of my sight...Sorry to worry you...I'll see you tomorrow night."

Dad hangs up the phone and I lay back down, pretending to be asleep. He walks back into the room and I feel the bed shake a little as he wiggles his way in between us. I feel him reach under me and he pulls me in tight. I crack my eye open and see Aidan across from me, wrapped up in Dad's other arm. Even if Dad can't see monsters, I know there's no way it could pry us from Dad's strong arms. My body starts to relax and I let go of the worry, the panic, the need to protect Aidan and the need to protect myself. I lay there, thinking about everything that's happened. I remember the monster pointing at us before it disappeared. Why did it do that and how did it get into the closet? Did it hide in our bag? Couldn't have. That monster was huge and the bag was so small. Then it must be the closet! Wait, we had closets at our old home and nothing showed up there. Why are Aidan and I the only ones that can see them? Rachel knows about them, but she said she could only feel the "Cellar Dweller". She never saw it. What was Dad talking about on the phone? "I don't believe in all that mumbo jumbo". What mumbo jumbo? I know he was talking to Mama, who else knows the best way to calm us down? Dad said he didn't believe in the mumbo jumbo…but Mama does! Everything that's happened started when we moved into that crummy old house. Kokotilo Manor! Rachel said that the kids in town know it's haunted and even she's heard the weird sounds coming from behind the purple-stone walls. But we're not at the Manor now, we're at Dad's apartment…then it hits me. I think about the green monster pointing at us, the Shadows on the playground, the "Cellar Dweller"…Dad couldn't see the monster, neither could the kids on the playground. The Shadows haven't bothered Mama and Rachel can only hear noises, and feel the monster's presence. Everything that's happened has brought Aidan and I face to face with the Shadows…it's not the house that's haunted, it's us!

(the eleventh scroll)

Not long after D-day (divorce day), I got called to the office at my old school. I'd never been called to the office before, so I thought maybe they'd found the gloves I lost before Christmas or I'd won some sort of prize. I was so excited that I ran down the hall, but when I got to the office, Mrs. Bunsen, the school secretary, looked at me as if something horrible had happened. She told me to have a seat on the bench and the smile on my face was quickly erased. I instantly thought about my Mama and Dad, and how Sandy Evans got called to the office last year when his Mom was in a car crash. My legs started bouncing up and down so fast that the bench banged against the wall. After what seemed like forever, Mrs. Bunsen's phone rang. She answered it, and kept her eyes on me the whole time she talked. "Uh-huh." she said, "He's right here. Okay." She hung up the phone and pointed at Principal Chan's office. I slowly got up and walked to the door. I stopped just outside, afraid of what Mr. Chan had to tell me. Behind me I heard Mrs. Bunsen say, "Go on." I took a deep breath and opened the door. As the door slowly opened I saw

Mama and Dad sitting there, across from Mr. Chan. "Hey." I said surprised and relieved that they were okay. But if they are both here, then something must have happened to Aidan! "What's wrong? Where's Aidan?" Mr. Chan got up, put a chair between Mama and Dad for me and motioned for me to sit down. As I sat down, Mr. Chan pulled out a couple of textbooks. They were the same textbooks I had in my class. Mr. Chan, still silent, opened the science book and pointed to the name on the inside cover. It was mine. He raised his eyebrows and I nodded agreeing it was my book. He then turned to a picture of a scientist holding beakers. He cleared his throat, wiggled his mustache and asked, "Would you like to explain this?" I looked at the picture closer and suddenly I knew what he was talking about. On the bottom left side of the picture, on top of the table with the beakers on it, there was a drawing of a pile of poop. Mr. Chan then opened my math book and like my science textbook, hidden in a bunch of pictures, were more drawings of poop. Every textbook he opened had more of the same, page after page, pile after pile of poop. There was poop on everything.

Poop on division questions, poop on maps, poop on grammar and my personal favorite, poops throughout history. I started laughing and the mustache on Mr. Chan's stone face started to twitch. My Mama grabbed my wrist and squeezed it hard, telling me to stop. Mr. Chan was so frustrated that his mustache was basically dancing under his nose. He cleared his throat again and said," Can you explain all this?"" I'm sorry." I said, my voice cracking, trying my best to hold back a giggle," My parents are getting a divorce." With those words, my giggle stopped instantly." And things have been pretty crummy around home lately... I was just trying to make myself laugh." Mr. Chan stared at me. His mustache stopped twitching, but his eyes still meant business. He leaned forward and said, "These are school property and writing in them is vandalism." " All the poop was done in pencil." I said in my defense." I can erase it all." Mr. Chan picked up the history book and looked at it. He flipped the pages and suddenly stopped on a page in the middle. I'm not sure what picture he was looking at, but it must have been a bad one, because his face got really red." Pencil?" he blurted, his voice now really straining. "I don't agree with any of the graffiti in your math, science or English books..." He looked up at me with tears in his eyes, "but this guy definitely deserved it!" He burst out laughing and turned the book around. The page he was staring at was a true classic, some of my best work. On top of a picture of Adolf Hitler I'd drawn a very large poop hat, complete with steam. Dad, Mama and I began laughing too! I laughed so hard I almost pee'd my pants and the four of us kept on laughing for a good five minutes. When we all finally calmed down, Mr. Chan said I was never to tell anyone about Poop-a-polooza, because he didn't want a bunch of copycats wrecking their own textbooks. For the next two weeks, I had detention everyday after school in Mr. Chan's office. Page by page I had to erase all the poops and although my wrist got sore from all the erasing, it was worth it, because I got what I wanted. In the middle of all the sadness, surrounding my parent's divorce; I got to have one heck of a laugh.

I wish I could make everyone laugh right now, because when Dad dropped us off back at the Manor, Mama told him they needed to talk and made us go upstairs. I know this has something to do with Dad's phone call last night, but even though Aidan and I are sitting on the top stair, so far I haven't been able to hear much.

"Pashawn?" Aidan says to me, he looks worried.

"Don't worry. They're probably just arranging all the stuff for our next visit to Dads." I say, but Aidan knows it isn't true, because we hear Dad's voice getting louder.

A few seconds later he starts yelling and we can understand every word.

"Why would you do that? Whatever you say happened, it was a long time ago. There's no blessed way I'm going to allow you to expose our kids to it!"

Mama raises her voice too, but uses a soft tone, trying to calm him down.

"Please. It's the only person I know that can handle this. I know it sounds crazy, but I know what I saw. Trust me, it's the only way."

"Trust you?" Dad yells and Mama yells back.

"Yeah, there's a first time for everything!"

It was just like when they used to fight. Their voices get louder and louder. I can hear Dad banging things and stomping his feet. I look over and Aidan is shaking. He's covering his ears with his mittens and rocking back and forth. We hear Dad's loud footsteps stomping out of the living room, so I pull Aidan in tight and crouch down on the top stair. Dad throws the front door open.

He's now screaming at the top of his lungs.

"Fine, have it your way, but if they end up anymore screwed up than they already are, you'll be hearing from my lawyer!"

"EEEEERRRRRAAAAAAHHHH!!!!" A dark scream comes from deep inside Aidan and he takes off down the stairs.

"Stop Aidan!" I yell and run after him.

He bolts for the front doors and Dad tries to step in front of him. Aidan runs faster, puts his head down like a football player and knocks Dad right off his feet. As my Dad flies through the air and bangs into the wall, Aidan runs out the door and disappears into the garden.

"Nice work!" I yell at Dad and Mama. "You were supposed to stop fighting. That's the whole reason you ruined our family, right? Because of you guys, Aidan barely speaks. Who knows what you've done to him now! I hate your fighting and I hate you both!"

Before they can say a word back to me, I run out the door and into the bushes of the dark garden.

As I get deeper and deeper into the thick gardens, the

calls of my parents, telling us to come back, get quieter and the gardens start to look more like a forest. The bushes get bigger, the trees get bigger and before I know it, I can no longer hear my parents' voices. Only a faint twinkle of sunlight pierces through the heavy trees and bushes, making it look more like midnight than noon.

"Aidan?" I call out. "Aidan! It's just me!"

I know he's a fast runner, but he couldn't have gotten too far ahead of me. I'm sure he's just around the next tree, or the next one, or the next. All the trees and bushes start to look the same and I can't tell if I've been running straight or in circles, so I stop. In all directions there's nothing but grey, twisted trees and bushes with sharp thorns. There is no point in running anymore. Even if I sprint, I don't know what direction he ran in. He could be anywhere and if he is still covering his ears there is no way he'll hear me through those thick mittens. Which way would he go? Well, Aidan always makes an "L" with his thumb and finger to know his right from left, so I pick left and start walking. The sharp thorns make every step I take painful and as the brush gets thicker, I'm starting to think that Aidan couldn't have come this way. There are no tracks, no broken branches and the thorns would be too much for him. Where is he? The image of the monster in Dad's closet flashes across my mind. I see it pointing at us.

"Aidan!...Aidan!"

I start walking back. Well, what I think is back, desperate to find Aidan before the Shadows do. As I walk through the dark woods, I start hearing branches breaking on my right. Probably just a squirrel or something, but as I walk on, the breaking sound gets louder. Those branches sound way to big for a squirrel to break.

"Aidan?" I whisper, but no answer.

I stop and crouch down behind bush. I try to see what's out there, but the bushes are too thick to see anything through. Whatever it is, I'll let it pass and if it's Aidan, then I'll grab him and we can get out of here. But, go where? There is no way I'm taking him back to the Manor, with Mama and Dad fighting. We can't stay out here for too long. These woods are scary enough in the daytime. I can only imagine what monsters come out in the dark. Monsters! That's right. They're hunting us. There's nowhere we can be safe. We? Aidan is all alone! I jump to my feet and yell "Monster!"

I bound through the thick thorns, screaming with rage! If that is a monster out there in the woods, I'm taking him out before he finds Aidan! Up ahead of me I see a thick branch laying on the ground. I'm not sure what happened to me, but suddenly I'm diving through the air towards it. Like the night in Mama's room, my body flips, end-over-end and lands softly.

As if I'd been practicing this my whole life, I roll along the mossy ground, grab the branch and spring to my feet. My shoes are barely touching the ground I'm running so fast, but it's not just my body that's acting weird. Behind the trees ahead, I see a Shadow move and as I point the branch towards it, the thick, sharp bushes in front of me seem to part, like they're clearing a path for me. But there is no time to figure this out because the Shadow is getting away and suddenly I'm not scared at all. With the bushes bending before me, I'm able to catch up to the Shadow in seconds. Only a few trees separate us as I run beside it, but I still can't make out exactly what it is. The one thing I do know is it's time to take this thing down. I leap into the air, use my feet to spring off a tree trunk and land smack dab in front of it. I grab the branch with both hands and raise it above my head. I step into the swing, like a baseball player, making sure the first strike counts and as the branch whistles through the air the Shadow screams, "CAAAIIILUUUMMM!!!!"

At the last second I let go of the branch, sending it flying through the air. The heavy branch slams into a tree trunk at least a hundred feet away and explodes into a million pieces.

"What the heck were you trying to do? Kill me?" The Shadow says as it steps forward into a ray of light.

"Rachel? What are you doing out here?"

She puts her hands on her hips, which tells me she is not

happy.

"After what happened at school I haven't had a chance to talk to you, so I came by to see you. But that stupid gate of yours wouldn't open."

"Yeah it kinda has a mind of it's own." I joke, knowing full well it's true.

"So, I had to climb over the wall." she says as if it was no big deal.

"There's no way. That wall is ten feet high!" I say and she looks at me puzzled.

"Do I look like some kind of prissy girl to you?"

"No." I say immediately.

"Good." She continues, "Anyway, I thought I was walking towards the driveway, but before I knew it I was lost. Clearly you guys need a gardener."

I look around, "Aidan's lost too, that's why I'm out here. He's alone. I've got to keep looking for him."

I start walking and Rachel catches up to me.

"Good thing I showed up, cause I've seen you try to find construction paper…"

I smile. "Yeah this time lets find the paper, not the monster."

We laugh a little and start to bash our way deeper into the forest.

"Aidan! Aidan!" Rachel and I call out as we move through the woods. It must have been an hour since we started walking and I'm starting to getting really worried.

"What if we don't find him?" I say under my breath.

Rachel whispers, "We will." I'm so glad she's here with me and I hope she's right.

"What was so important that you had to climb a wall to tell me." I ask and out of the corner of my eye, I notice she's blushing.

"I just wanted to say that what you did for your brother, on the playground, was really great. I mean you didn't care about being teased or anything. You really love your brother and…"

She grabs my arm, stopping me.

I turn and she's staring at me. Her eyes look somehow, bigger.

She leans in and…

"Pashawn, Pashawn!" I hear Aidan, teasing me, and Rachel pulls away.

"Aidan!" she screams and picks him up in her arms like a big sister.

"Are you okay?" I ask and she sets him down.

"Sashawn." he says.

"Well you're safe now." I pull down the puppy hood on his pajamas and hold his little head in my hands.

161

"I know that fighting scared you, but it's over. It's not our fault they're jerks." I tell him and he grabs my hand and starts pulling me.

"Whoa, where are you going?" I say, stopping him.

He points, "Pashawn Pea!"

"Wait, you know the way out?"

"Sashawn Pea." He nods his head and then pats me on the back, "Pashawn, Sashawn."

"All this time, you've been looking for me? Well I'm sure glad you found me, but we're not going back to the Manor. Mama and Dad are there."

He points again, "Sashawn!"

I look at him and his little face looks so dirty, tired and hungry. That's when I start to realized just how exhausted I am.

"Alright." I sigh, "We'll go back, but I'm not talking to either of them."

Aidan nods and we follow him into the woods.

As we walk through the woods, they become more and more garden like, the tall trees get smaller and the bushes, less thorny. Soon, through the twisted trees, I can see the Manor, up ahead. We will hit the driveway in a few feet and I'm sure Rachel will want to get going home. I look forward and ask her casually, "So back in the woods, you were saying something to me about Aidan and the playground..."

"Right." She say's still looking ahead also. "I wanted to tell you that the other kids thought what you did was pretty cool too, so they decided that you're no longer P.U.'d."

"Great." I say and although I'm happy to not be P.U.'d anymore, it's not exactly what I was hoping to hear.

Aidan jumps over the last of the bushes and runs up the driveway. I see Mama and Dad run down from the porch towards us. As we step out to the driveway I turn to Rachel and say, "thanks for helping me find Aidan and for being a friend."

Rachel steps in front of me, "that's the other thing I wanted to tell you..." she whispers, "I want you to be my boyfriend."

Like before, in the woods she leans in, only this time her lips touch mine! My legs go weak and I almost fall down. I'm sure it was just a second or two but it felt like forever. I feel her lips pull away from mine and I open my eyes. Mama and Dad are standing a few feet away looking stunned, with their jaws dropped wide open.

"Hi there." Rachel says and walks up to them.

"Hello" they both reply, still standing stiff, as if they've just seen a ghost.

"It's a pleasure to meet you both. I'm Rachel." she says and Mama's eyes light up.

"Oh, you're Rachel." Mama says with a giggle in her voice,

"I've heard a lot about you…"

I clear my throat, telling her to stop and she cuts her sentence short.

"…it's a pleasure to meet you too."

My Dad is now smiling too and looking at me proud, as if I won a race or something. There's a very long, awkward silence. Dad stares at me, Mama smiles weirdly at Rachel and Aidan runs in circles around us all. I was considering pretending to faint until Rachel broke the silence.

"You have a very interesting house, Mrs. Kokotilo…"

My Mama's smile disappears.

She looks at my Dad and then says quickly, "It's Ms. and thank you. Would you like to come in? You have all been out here for a while, I'm sure you're hungry."

Oh crackers, no! I can't take an hour of Mama and Dad staring at us and making stupid smiley faces. It's gross.

"Rachel was just saying that she needed to get home…" I blurt out and Rachel follows my lead.

"Yeah. I really can't stay, I just came by to tell Cailum that he's my boyfriend now."

Boom! It's like a Kid-Parent bomb went off! What is Rachel thinking…T.M.I., Rachel, T.M.I!!! My Mama starts to shake and giggle, my Dad is practically exploding from puffing his chest out with pride and even throws out an "Atta Boy!" The barrier between kid and parent worlds has been breached, there is no turning back and I am now really gonna faint…for real!

I feel something cold and wet on my face and open my eyes. Mama is standing over me.

"There's my little bear." she whispers.

I look around and realize that I'm laying in Mama's bed.

"Where's Rachel?" I ask and sit straight up.

Mama tilts her head to the side.

"She's gone home. Your Dad gave her a ride."

"He left? I didn't say goodbye."

Mama puts on one of her concerned smiles.

"Honey, you were in and out for about an hour. He had to get going, to beat the Sunday traffic, but he said he would call you later and check up on you. You can say goodbye then. Now listen, you are very dehydrated and hungry so, when you're ready, I want you to come down to the kitchen." She kisses me on the head and walks out of the room.

What a day. Mama and Dad fighting, Aidan being lost, Rachel kissing me…oh crackers, I'm so embarrassed. I can't believe Rachel kissed me and then I fainted right in front of her. Just then Mama pokes her head back into the room.

"And don't worry about Rachel, she said she likes how sensitive you are. Apparently fainting is pretty cool to her."

Mama winks and walks away. Great, Mama sees Rachel

kiss me and they're pals.

By the time I reach the kitchen, Aidan is up to his knuckles in milk, and by the look of the mountain of crumbs around him, he's had at least four cookies already.

"There you are." Mama says and I just stare at her.

I've got all my wits back now and I remember how mad I am at her and Dad for fighting. I swore I wouldn't speak to either of them. I may have broken down for a second and talked to her upstairs, but that didn't count. I was out of it. Technically, she took advantage of my weakened state. But now I'm gonna stick to what I planned. I'm not talking to her and when my Dad calls, I'm not gonna talk to him either! The cookies on the table are just more fuel for my fire. I hate cookies, so I put on my best stone face, stomp to the table and flop down in a chair. Mama smiles at me and I look away. I'm not gonna let her think that because she put a wet cloth on my head, everything's forgiven. Mama gets up from the table.

"I know you're not big on cookies..." she says as she walks over to the fridge, "so I made you a pumpkin pie."

She opens the fridge and pulls out a deep dish, home made, fluffy pastry, pumpkin pie! I know it sounds weird, but I love pumpkin pie. Straight up. No whipped cream. I can resist just about anything, but this is my Kryptonite. Like a kid whacked out on gas at the dentist, I'm suddenly in a daze, sitting tall at the huge table and shoveling pumpkin pie into my mouth, without a care in the world. Spoonful after glorious spoonful. I dig into the deep pie and wiggle in my chair as I chew.

"So…" my Mama says.

With a mouthful of pie I reply, "Yes, Mama."

No! She did it again. I spoke to her! Is she some kind of brainwashing master? I drop my fork and reality suddenly slaps me in the face. Of course, Aidan's milk and cookies, and my pumpkin pie? They're classic "Talk" food. I try to beat her to the punch.

"Mama, Aidan's okay, so let's just forget about it. I really don't feel like talking."

"I'm sorry we fought honey. I promise I won't let it happen again, but that's not what I want to talk about." She says seriously.

"It's not?" I wonder.

"I want to talk about what happened at Dad's."

I quickly blow it off so she won't keep on talking and I can get back to my pie.

"It was nothing. Just a nightmare, okay?"

Mama's not letting this moment go so easily and she pulls a chair up between Aidan and I.

"Really?" she says, using that way of talking where she's half believing you and half digging deeper. She raises her eyebrows and continues, "Then what's all that in your bedroom? I know it's a fort, but why all the flashlights and glow sticks? And why is all that stuff stacked up in front of the closet? Unless you really hate clothes, the only reason I can think of to put a dresser in front of a closet is that you're afraid of something in it."

I try and play it down. "It's just a fort, Mama."

Mama sighs, "Boys, I know there has been some… things happening…things you don't understand…things that Dad and I don't even understand…and so I've asked for help… from someone very special, who does understand…to come and stay with us."

I get up and stomp towards the kitchen doors.

"This is all your fault. None of this happened until you took us away from our home and brought us to this crummy place. We don't need anyone to come and stay with us…we need DAD! He's supposed to protect us. He did when we all lived together. No one believes us…they are real!!!"

Mama stands up.

"Cailum, I believe you! The Shadows, the monsters… I've seen them too."

I stop dead in my tracks and Mama walks over to the greenhouse doors. She looks out them and sighs, "Honey, when I was your age, I saw them too…so did Marty."

Aidan knocks over his glass of milk and Mama jumps. She turns around and we all look at the milk, but do nothing to stop it and just let it pour onto the floor. As Mama watches the milk drip she says, "Boys, there are things all around us that only some people can see."

Mama looks at us and we all just stare at each other, because it's no longer a secret. She knows...she believes us. I should feel relieved, but I don't, I'm actually more scared than ever. As long as Mama and Dad didn't believe it, a part of me could pretend it wasn't real. That they weren't real...but now they are. Everything becomes so quiet, so still, I can hear Mama and Aidan breathing. Now that we have said it out loud, I'm afraid of what's next. Did they hear us? We all scan the room, our eyes watching, looking for any sign of them, waiting for the Shadows to come. BING! BONG! The doorbell rings!

"AAAAAHHHHHHH!" Aidan and I run out of the kitchen down the hall. As we reach the front foyer a crack of lightening flashes and there is a Shadow standing right outside the front glass door!

"AAAAAHHHHHHHH!!!" Another crack of lightening flashes and the Shadow starts banging on the glass.

"This is not a drill!" I yell, and in an instant we go into "Shadow Defense Mode." It's now time to put all of our practice and preparations into action! We leap over the bottom railing and race up the stairs. As I pass the picture of the old lady hanging on the wall, I grab it with both hands and spin it. The pulley and wires we attached to it opens our bedroom door down the hall.

"All clear" I shout and Aidan salutes me and we keep running.

When we reach our bedroom door I give the orders.

"Dive, dive!"

We dive through the doorway together and land at the base of our fort. This is exactly what we built this for!

"Climb, climb!" I then command and we both shoot up the ramp to the top bunk.

"Drop the stone!" I yell and Aidan rolls over to the right side of the bed, picks up a large stone with a rope attached to it and throws it over the side. The rope and pulley we built raises the ramp up, so now no invader can reach us.

"Crank the wheel!" I say, but Aidan is already a step ahead of me. As he spins the steering wheel from an old car, one of the pulleys slams the door shut while another moves heavy metal bars across it, locking it tight. Now last but not least I scream "Covers!" and we both dive under the blankets.

This isn't really a part of the fort's defenses, but hiding your head under covers really helps when you're scared. Everything then goes quiet. Eerily quiet, like when you're hiding in the basement, playing hide and seek and it's taking forever for someone to find you. So, we wait...and wait, but nothing happens. Time passes so slowly when you are hiding and even slower when you're hiding from terrifying Shadows.

Laying here waiting feels like forever. My body starts to cramp and my breathing starts to sound as loud as a jet engine. I can't take this for much longer so I whisper to Aidan.

"I think the coast is clear."

We're about to pull the covers back, when I hear noises coming from the hall.

"Pashawn Pea!" Aidan says scared and he pulls the hood on his P.J's over his head.

"It's okay." I tell him "With all those bars and locks, that door is impenetrable."

Aidan puts a mitten in front of my mouth, stopping me from talking. We both listen...

RATTLE, RATTLE, RATTLE.

"What was that?"

RATTLE, RATTLE, RATTLE.

Someone's turning the doorknob. Aidan and I hold our breath.

RATTLE, RATTLE, RATTLE...silence

"See. Impenetrable." I whisper to Aidan.

He gives me the thumbs up with his mitten. Then suddenly

we both hold our breath, because we hear a voice whisper:

"If I were them,

and they were me,

I wonder where,

I would be?"

The voice sounds close, too close. The floor creaks. The voice isn't coming from the hall…it's coming from inside our room! How did they get in here? I didn't hear any locks breaking or our door busting down. "Periscope" I mouth to Aidan. He quietly creeps over to the corner of the bunk bed and looks into the eyepiece of my homemade reverse periscope. He twists it around so that it's pointed at the door and then pulls away from the scope and mouths "Sashawn." I wiggle over beside him and take a look. As I slowly turn the periscope towards the door, I see what scared him so bad and I start to panic. There, between the door and the bed, is a pair of sparkling red running shoes. I turn the periscope a little more and I see the bottom of a craggily old stick. I mouth to Aidan "IT'S IN FRONT OF THE BED AND IT HAS A STICK TO HIT US WITH!!!!!" I pull a piece of string that I attached to the side of the periscope that moves the lenses in the bottom, so I can zoom in. I focus on the door. It's impossible! The large bars are all still in place and the door is shut tight! Whoever or whatever is standing in front of our bed got inside without breaking the locks or even opening the door!

All of a sudden the thing speaks again. The sound of it's voice is hypnotizing:

"Not a peep, or a whisper,

barely a sound.

I guess two little boys,

don't wish to be found.

I will wait for the honor,

I will not go far.

The Nana is ready,

whenever you are."

I look at Aidan and at the same time we both mouth the exact same thing, "The Nana?"

I look back into the periscope and in just those few seconds, it's disappeared. I zoom in on the door and it's still untouched. As I search the room for any sign of the red-shoed monster, it's voice seems to echo in my head. There's something strange about that voice. Not scary, but actually familiar. It's like I know it, but how could I?

"Pashawn?" Aidan asks.

"Hall vision. Great idea." I agree and open a wood box on the other side of the bunk bed.

Inside we put the old T.V. that's attached to a cell phone we hid in the hall. The phone is old, but it's camera and microphone still work great. We put on our earphones and watch the screen closely for any sign of movement. The hall is empty. Whatever was just in our room isn't hanging around. Maybe our fort's defenses were too much for it? Wait, there, in the corner of the screen I see Mama coming down the hall.

"Oh, no." I say to Aidan, "Mama doesn't know it's out there. We have got to warn her!"

Just as I'm about to pull my earphones off, Mama yells.

"Boys get out here, now."

Her voice is so loud it almost blows our earphones. Through the ringing in my ears, I think I can hear the voice of the monster again. Aidan points to his earphones and I nod. He hears it too. We both listen closely because it's voice is soft, we can barely hear it:

> *"It's okay, I can wait,*
> *all day and all night.*
> *The boys will come out,*
> *when the timing is right."*

The monster suddenly appears in the corner of the screen, but before we can get a good look at it, Mama steps in front of the camera, blocking our view. She steps towards the stranger.

"NO MAMA, RUN!!!" I yell but she must not be able to hear me because she keeps moving closer to the monster.

As she steps towards it I hear her say, "Thank you so much for coming. I didn't know who else to call."

What? Mama invited this monster into our house? Oh, no. They must have possessed her, gotten her under their control! Before I can release the pulley that opens the door to go out and save her, the strange monster replies:

"I'm here for you Nini,

family always comes first.

Strength comes from adversity,

a blessing out of a curse.

What's happened is in the past,

there is nothing we can do,

but history will not repeat itself,

I promise this to you.

Whatever is brewing,

be it wicked or wild,

I am here to protect you,

for you are my child."

Her child? Hold on...THAT'S OUR GRANDMA? I feel so stupid. Running away from an old lady, locking our door... wait, our door. Now it all starts to make sense. I get it, that's how she got in here. This was her house. I bet there are all kinds of secret doors in this place. I begin to feel angry. Not because an old lady tricked us, but because I realize that this is who Mama called to help us. Nice work Mama! Our grandmother, the magician, is going to save us from a five hundred pound, slimy monster and a thousand angry Shadows. I look back at the screen, as our grandmother's two, wrinkled old hands wrap around Mama's waist.

"Hug away, grandma." I say to Aidan, "Get your fill, cause you ain't pinching our cheeks."

Aidan laughs and then suddenly points to his earphones. I listen closely but I can't hear what's going on. I motion to Aidan and he turns the volume up as loud as it will go. Now I can hear. It's Mama's and she sounds worried.

"You know how their Dad feels about all this. I promised him you'd not involve them. So, please just fix this…that's all. Okay?"

Our Grandma clears her throat and replies:

"As always my dear,

I will do my best,

but just to reassure you,

the answer is yes."

I look closely at the wrinkled arms wrapped around Mama and notice that Grandma has her fingers crossed.

"I'm sorry, Ma, that the boys are being so rude." Mama says. "I'm sure that wasn't quite the welcome you were hoping for. Ma, you look a little tired. I know it was a long trip. Do you want me to take you to your room? "

Grandma lets go of Mama's waist and she says:

"You are right my dear,

it has been a long day.

No need to show me though,

I know the way.

My strength grows weary,

I'll go get some rest.

There is much work to be done,

I must be at my best."

"Again with the rhyming." I say to Aidan, "Must be some kind of old person disease. Dr. Seuss-itus. She's totally lost her marbles!"

As they turn around to walk down the hall, Aidan and I get our first full look at our weird, rhyming Grandma. First of all, she's short, really short, in fact I'm sure Aidan's taller than her. She has grey hair with streaks of black in it and it's pulled up tight on top of her head. It makes her look kinda like a senior sumo wrestler. Her face is really wrinkly and she has round glasses with red lenses. Her skin is completely pale except for her rosy red cheeks. She has a shiny, yellow robe on that's so big that it hangs off of her tiny, fragile body like a dress. As if that wasn't weird enough, she's wearing sparkling, red, old school basketball shoes and long white socks that go all the way up to her knobby little knees. She probably thought wearing teenager's shoes would make us think she was cool or something. Right Grandma, you would have had us fooled if it weren't for your cane…Pwned! I bet she has a cane, because she can fall over at anytime, like a baby. Only this baby has really brittle bones. Great, with all the stairs in this place, I'm gonna be on Grandma-sitting duty twenty-four/seven. I don't want to be held responsible if this old lady, that I don't even know, falls and shatters her bones into a million tiny pieces. Maybe we can get her one of those electronic monitoring devices. Then if she falls, an alarm will go off and the ambulance can come and pick her up off the floor. I look at her on the screen, so old and wrinkly, wobbling along on that stupid cane. That cane. There is something strange about that cane. I can't stop staring at it. It's twisty and knotted and the hook at the top fits perfectly into her hand. Canes are usually made of dead wood, but this one looks like it's still living. It's color is a bright yellow-brown and it looks like it has bits of green on it, like tiny leaves. Even though her outfit is absolutely crazy, that cane keeps holding my stare. It feels almost familiar, but how could it? I've never seen this woman until today. Suddenly a strong feeling takes over me. All through my body I feel it pulling me, like the toy section at a department store. I look at Aidan and notice that he's also staring wide-eyed at her cane. Through my earphones, I hear a voice. It's her voice, not soft this time, but loud and strong. It's so loud that I pull off my headphones, but I can still hear her. I look around, but it isn't in our room. Where is her voice coming from? A secret door again? I put my hands over my ears, to block out the sound, but still I hear her...I look at the screen and there she is still wobbling down the hall. She's not in the room, or hiding behind a secret door...she's in my head!

"You think you may want it,

but that is only half true.

The Shadows desire the cane,

and they are trying to use you."

"She just spoke to me in my head!" I gasp at Aidan and he points at himself.

"Sashawn."

"You heard her too?" I ask and he nods.

What did she mean about the Shadows using me? Why would they want her cane? I look at the cane again on the screen and I realize what is so familiar about it and why the Shadows would want it. It's made of the same twisted wood as the tree in the greenhouse and the posts of our bunk bed. I know that wood has the power to scare the Shadows away, so does that mean she can scare them away too? Holy fish crackers! That's not the worst of it. It's not the cane that makes me suddenly sick to my stomach or the Shadows, it's her voice...I've heard her voice before, I know it. It was her voice I heard in my head when we were driving away from our old home and the same one that spoke to me when I found the book in the greenhouse! This is not your average Grandma! She can walk through walls, destroy Shadow monsters with her cane and read people's minds...Oh, no...no...NO! Does that mean she's heard all the things I said about her? All those bad things...about being old and wrinkly... her stupid cane, falling down like a baby and losing her mind! Her voice whispers in my head.

"Yes my dear.

Let me give you some advice.

Your thoughts are stronger than words,

so you should try to be nice!"

Forget about the monsters or the Shadows...my Grandma is totally gonna kill me!

to eto ellse

(the twelfth scroll)

Mental Telepathy is the power to send and receive thoughts or feelings with other people using only your mind. I read a story about Mental Telepathy online, at "Unexplained and Unnatural.com." It's a website about people with paranormal powers. The story was about twin brothers, Carl and Chris, who could talk to each other using their minds. This came in pretty handy because they didn't learn to speak until they were ten. They also used their Mental Telepathy to talk to their older brother Ted, so he could tell people what they wanted or needed, kind of like a translator. Their parents said that Chris and Carl would all of a sudden start laughing, like they were telling each other jokes, or start fighting without even being in the same room. What really scared the parents was that the boys seemed to be able to read their minds too. Their father said that one day he was changing the oil on their car, laying underneath it and needed a specific type of wrench. Just as he realized the wrench wasn't close enough for him to grab, Carl showed up out of nowhere, holding the exact wrench his father needed. They said that the boys were never surprised on their birthdays, because they already knew what they were getting. After they learned to speak, this power still came in handy, like when they were writing tests at school they could tell each other the answers or read a girl's mind and find out if she liked them or not. As they got older, they started to use their power less and less and Ted no longer needed to translate for them. By the time they were in their twenties, Carl and Chris had pretty much forgotten how to use it. Until one day, when Carl got a phone call from Chris' wife saying that Chris was missing. Carl said that all of a sudden he got a strong feeling that Chris was in danger. He called the police, but they said that Chris needed to be missing for 24 hours before they could begin a search, so Carl jumped into his car and went out to find him on his own. Carl said that he didn't know exactly where his brother was, but as he drove, he began hearing Chris' voice in his head. At first it was soft, but the more he concentrated on it, the clearer it got. Soon he said it was like he was talking to Chris on the phone, telling him how far to drive and where to turn. Left, right, straight, Carl kept driving for over an hour and finally, on an old dirt road, he saw Chris' car, upside down in the ditch. He ran over and pulled Chris out of the car, just in time, because as he got his brother just a few feet away, Chris' car exploded.

At the scene of the accident, the police found traces of hundred dollar bills scattered all over, but because they were so burnt, they were untraceable. Chris was taken to the hospital and after a few weeks he made a full recovery, but was unable to explain why he was driving down that old dirt road and where the burnt money came from. If that wasn't weird enough, what the doctors told Carl really confused him. They said that Chris had hit his head so hard on the dash during the accident, that he had been unconscious for hours. Which means that he couldn't have told Carl where to find him. Carl couldn't figure out whose voice had been guiding him that night. Was it just luck or was it something else? After he got out of the hospital, Chris started to act really strange and later that year he was arrested for robbing a bank. Carl thought that maybe the accident had caused some sort of brain damage, or maybe the pills the doctor's gave Chris had made him go crazy. Unable to make sense of his brother's crazy behavior, Carl went to visit Chris in jail and asked him why he'd done it? All Chris said was," Because Ted told me to!"

Hours passed and we stayed held up in our bunk bed fort. Our bodies may have been safe, but our minds were now open to invasion. Every time I've thought of something I had to ask myself, "Is this my thought or is "The Nana" wiggling around in my head." I think Aidan is having the same problem. He just stares at the wall and every once in a while he shakes his head, like he was trying to get something out of it. I soon realize that hearing her voice in our heads wouldn't make us go crazy, but worrying about her reading our minds would.

"We gotta stop this." I say to Aidan and he agrees.
"She's an old lady, she's not the Boogie Man. For all we know, every old person can use Mental Telepathy. Think about it. How many other old people do we know?"

Aidan scratches his head and then shrugs his shoulders.

"None. Right? And the only thing bad about what she said to us was the rhyming. Okay, that's it then. From now on, no more acting crazy."

I pull out a couple of old hockey helmets we found in the room when we were building the fort.

"Put this on. It's an extra layer of protection…just in case."

We both put them on. They smell like moldy puzzles and are way too big for us, but they help us stop worrying about "The Nana", so we keep them on.

We stayed in our room for the rest of the evening, talking and playing all the body part wars; blinking wars, thumb wars, leg wars and we even invented a new one, nose wars. That one really hurt, so it only lasted one round. When Mama called us for dinner, we didn't go, but as it got darker outside our stomachs started to growl. So far we had managed to hole up in our room, but now there was problem. Food, the one flaw in our plan.

How could I not have prepared for this? "Think, think." I keep saying to myself, trying to figure out a way to get some food in here, and keep "The Nana" out, but I can't come up with anything.

I turn to Aidan, defeated, "I'm afraid we are gonna have to leave the room."

He looks at me scared then suddenly shouts, "Pashawn Pea."

He releases the pulley and the ramp drops down.

"Sashwan!" he yells and runs down it.

I get up, walk down the ramp and find Aidan rooting through one of the boxes we stuffed under the bed.

"Stop." I tell him, "We need those under there for protection."

Aidan turns around and holds up a plastic bag.

"Pashawn Pea!!"

He tears the bag open, spilling a stash of old Halloween

candy all over the floor. Normally I'd be angry that he was hoarding candy, but not now.

My eyes light up and I cheer "Right on bro!"

Even if it's a few months old, it's still candy and we are starving. We sit on the floor and have a bedroom picnic, filling our bellies with sugar and chips. After devouring many pieces of old hard candy and stale chips, Aidan and I suddenly stop. We both gasp and fall back onto the floor, holding our tummies. Here is the thing about candy and chips. One is great, two is good, but a belly full is sickening, and a belly full of old candy is serious trouble! Like, Def-Con 4 trouble. We roll back and forth on the floor moaning and groaning, while our stomachs make horrible noises. All of a sudden, Aidan sits up and looks at me, his face is green and sweaty.

"Paaaashaaaawn" he moans and I know exactly what he means, because I'm feeling it too.

"We are going to have to go to the bathroom, Aidan." I say but Aidan just shakes his head no. "Yes, we do and we better go quick, because I don't know if I can hold it!

I barely get the last few words out before I have to put my hand over my mouth. I'm doing my best, trying to hold it back, but one way or another it's coming out and it's sure to be an epic barf. I stumble over to the wall, release one of the pulleys unlocking all the bars on the door and motion to Aidan with my other hand to follow. We open the door slowly and I poke my head out. I'm still covering my mouth as I check the hall to see if the coast is clear. I know that if I let go of my lips for one second it could cause barf-o-rama, like dominoes, first me, then Aidan, then me again. Oh, all this barf talk is gonna make me lose it! We quickly and quietly creep down the hall to the bathroom. Every step I take sends waves of sickness through my stomach. Even when the Shadows were chasing me, the bathroom never seemed so far away. Finally, we get to the bathroom door and Aidan taps me on the shoulder. I turn around to give him the stink eye, telling him that I'm first, but stop when I see what he's trying to tell me. Down at the very end of the hall, a strange blue light is shining out of the cracks of "The Nana's" door. It's no normal light. It's thick and moves like waves in the ocean, only these waves cling to the walls and ceiling. The thick light starts to move, spilling out through the cracks in her door, into the hall and quickly towards us. Aidan and I turn to run, but before we can take a step, the blue light is already surrounding us. I'm definitely scared, but strangely I don't feel sick any more and Aidan's face is no longer green. We both stand there stunned, looking at the blue light all around us. As it moves, it changes like globs of oil paint and bright sparkles swirl around in it like fireflies. Now, not only am I no longer feeling sick, I'm not scared either. The sparkles in the light all move in towards

189

each other and form bright blue orbs. They seem to dance with each other as they spin around Aidan and I. One of the orbs passes right through Aidan and he giggles, then another one goes through me. It feels like it's tickling me, from the inside and I start to giggle too. They come close to us and then move away, like they want to play, trying to get us to chase them. One of the orbs keeps circling Aidan and he keeps trying to grab it. It bobs and weaves out of the way, but Aidan finally gets his mittens on it. He holds it in his hands, staring at with huge smile, his face lit up by it's blue light, then, as if it was speaking to him, he nods and releases it. The orb circles him once more then shoots down the hall, stopping just outside of "The Nana's" door. Before I can stop him, Aidan chases after it, so I run after him. When I catch up to Aidan, the orb disappears through the "The Nana's" door.

"Come on." I say to Aidan, grabbing him by the arm.

Suddenly, an orb comes back out through the door, grabs onto Aidan's other arm. Now the orb and I are in a tug of war, with Aidan as the rope. I guess I'm stronger than I think, because after a few tugs, the orb lets go. Somehow that seems a little too easy. I may be strong, but it is clearly magic. That's when I notice that floating inside the orb is one of Aidan's mittens!

"Give it back." I order the orb and but it just floats there. Then, I swear it laughs and suddenly disappears again, back through the door, taking Aidan's mitten with it

"Forget about it. Let's go." I say to Aidan and start walking, but Aidan's having none of it.

He pulls away from me and runs back to the door.

"What are you doing? Let's go." I say and try to move him but he won't budge. He then holds up his mitten-less hand and looks at me with those big, sad, puppy dog eyes. Just like pumpkin pie, I'll do anything for those sad eyes.

"Fine." I say, "I'll get your mitten, but then we're out of here. Okay?"

I'll have to sneak in like a commando, on my belly and crawl so that she won't detect me. I get down on my hands and knees and crawl towards the door. As I slither on the floor towards it, I start to wonder, how am I going to open it? All of the doors in this old house squeak. And what if it's locked? Suddenly, the door opens a crack. I stop and look back at Aidan and he motions for me to keep going. I take a deep breath and gently nudge the door with my head so that it opens just enough for me to stick my head through.

I poke my head in and am blinded by a flash of bright light. As I try to see through the flash of light for any sign of Aidan's mitten, I feel him climb up on my back. This is no time to argue with him, so I let him stay there. After the few seconds of blinding light, it begins to fade. My eyes adjust and there, in the middle of the room, is "The Nana." She's not sleeping, but I wish she was because what she is doing is totally freaking me out!!! She is floating in the air, high above the floor and the blue light that spilled into the hall looks like it is coming out her chest! Yeah, that's right...floating. Like a cloud! With blue light shooting out of her! This is totally EPIC!

Her legs are crossed and her eyes are closed, like she's in some kind of trance. She starts to hum and the furniture in her room begins to fly around her! Her humming changes and what was only her voice sounds like a hundred. It gets stronger and stronger and the floor begins to shake. As the humming gets louder, I see her cane float up into the air. The orbs that played with us in the hall and stole Aidan's mitten now are swirling around her at lightning speed. Suddenly, the walls and floor start to peel towards us, like the skin of a banana and behind them, multi-colored clouds burst like fireworks. The clouds bang together, sending sparkles shooting through the air, that turn into beautiful flowers when they land on the ground. I look over to my right and see Aidan's mitten on a little chunk of what's left of the floor, just a few feet away. If we hang around in here much longer, there isn't gonna be a room left. She may even tear the whole house apart, so now is my only chance. I crawl quickly over, with Aidan still on my back, grab it, and make a dash for the door. We get to the door and I stand up, and start to run. Crawling is for creeping; running is for "Get the heck outta here!" Aidan holds on to my back and I run to our room, piggy backing him the whole way. Once inside, we spin the wheels and pull the pulleys, locking the door and raising the ramp. High up on the top bunk we dive under the covers and pull them over our heads.

"Did that really just happen?" I say to Aidan. "We gotta get outta here, tonight. This place is crazy and we are crazy if we stay here!"

Through the blanket I see something glowing and it isn't a flashlight. I pull the covers down just enough for one eye to peak out of. Up near the ceiling an orb is floating. I slowly pull the covers back over my head. Maybe it didn't see us. Maybe it will just go away? It hovers over the bed for a few seconds and then I see it fly away.

"That was close." I mouth to Aidan and we both just lay there, silent for a few minutes. After a little while we slowly pull the covers down to take a peek and make sure it's gone. We pop our heads out of the blanket and just as we hoped there is no orb anywhere. Aidan and I sit up and take a few deep breaths. The air under the blanket gets stale fast and we did eat a lot of candy old candy, so the stink factor under there was high! Suddenly, we hear a loud clap and out of nowhere, the orb appears and shoots straight towards us!

(the thirteenth scroll)

There was this kid at my old school named Peter Jenson, who was always getting into trouble and it was always his fault. He was just one of those kids that didn't like school and he really didn't like our fourth grade teacher Mrs. Slangly. I didn't think she was all that bad, but something about her and Peter didn't mix. Everyday he would act up and everyday she would give him detention. That went on for most of the year and then suddenly, after spring break, it stopped. Peter didn't act up in class at all and because of that he didn't get detention anymore. For the rest of the year, there was peace in Mrs. Slangly's class, that is, until days before summer holidays.

I went into the classroom early, to drop off my backpack. No one was there yet and so I walked straight to the cloakroom at the front of the class. As I hung up my backpack, I heard some noise coming from the classroom, so I went out to see who it was. At the back of the classroom, standing at Mrs. Slangly's desk, I saw Peter. I figured he was just handing in some homework, so I was about to say hi, when he started making this weird sound. At first it sounded like he was choking, then it sounded like he had something in his throat and finally it sounded grossly familiar. After making the noises, he hung his head over her coffee cup and what I saw next, I wish I'd never seen.

From his lips he dangled a huge lugie, the slimy kind that jiggles when it hits the ground. He let it hang there for a second and then dropped it right into her coffee cup! If that wasn't bad enough, he then picked up her spoon and stirred it in. He smiled with pride and then turned to walk out of the class and as he did he caught me standing there, watching him. "You aren't gonna tell are you?" he asked all nervous. I thought about it for a second and then realized that if he can spit in her coffee, who knows what gross stuff he could do to me? "No." I replied, "Besides, it's the end of the year, one time's not gonna kill her." Peter laughed, "One time? Nah, I've been spitting in her coffee for months. The school counsellor said I needed to do something to release my anger, or I would keep getting detention." I looked at him confused," He told you to spit in her coffee?" Peter raised his head, proud" Nah, that one was my idea." He patted me on the back and then walked out of the room. With only a few days left, I was able to keep his secret, but on the last day of school Mrs. Slangly walked up to the front of the class and called Peter's name. Peter looked at me. I shook my head to tell him I didn't snitch. Seriously though, what was he thinking? His lugies were so huge, sooner or later she was gonna see one floating in her cup. She's gonna fail him, I thought to myself, as he walked up to the front with his head down. When he finally got up to the chalkboard, Mrs. Slangly said," We all know Peter has been a trouble maker...but never, in a million years, did I think you'd do this..." Here it comes, I thought and I waited for her to start yelling, but instead she pulled out a bunch of flowers and handed them to him." You did it Peter! You are the most improved student I've ever had the privilege to teach. The flowers are to remind you to keep growing as you move forward into grade five." She then did something I have never seen a teacher do before. She hugged him and the whole class cheered. When she let go of him, Peter was burst into tears." I know Peter." Mrs. Slangly said, " I'm going to miss you next year as well. But no matter what, always know that I believe in you." Peter looked up at her, his body was shaking and tears were running down his face. Mrs. Slangly told him," It's okay Peter, just say how you feel." Peter cheeks blew up, his face went bright red and then he burst out," I spit in your coffee!!!"

I learned two valuable lessons that day. One, don't spit in people's coffee. Two, the people that make you so mad that you would want to spit in their coffee, sometimes end up giving you flowers.

I wake up to the sound of Aidan snoring and realize not only did I sleep through the night, but also that I'm hugging Aidan. Man, I can't remember ever sleeping this well. That orb must have knocked us out. Wait, that orb. Did any of that stuff even happen? Maybe it was all that old candy, causing us to see things. I look around the room, to see if there are any signs of the orb and notice that the curtains are glowing. Normally the dull gardens and fog that hangs around this old Manor, makes the light outside grey, but the curtains are lit up like a thousand watt bulb is pointing at them. Is it sunny outside? Holy fish crackers, video games and WiFi, it's the sun! I haven't seen sunshine since we moved here. I release the pulley and lower the ramp so I can go check it out. When I open the curtains I have to pinch myself, because I must still be dreaming. Ouch, that hurts! This is no dream! I run to the bedroom door, release the pulley, which unlocks the bars, and run down the hall. I leap down the stairs, two at a time and whip open the front door. Like when Rachel kissed me, my knees go weak and I can barely catch my breath. I slowly step out onto the front porch and what I see all around me is nothing short of a miracle!

The dull stones that made up the long driveway are now a brilliant shiny purple. Lemon-yellow grass lines the driveway and the grey, twisted trees are now ruby red, like "The Nana's" shoes. Below them blue-green bushes blow in the wind, like ocean waves. Every available branch and inch of the garden is now in full bloom with the bright, beautiful, odd shaped flowers, the kind Mama used to grow beside our front walk. Everywhere I look, in every garden that was once dead, I now see life and colors so wonderful, it makes my heart feel warm. A gust of wind blows over the bushes and trees and as the bright leaves and flowers rustle I hear them whisper "The Nana."

I run back into the house, not because I'm scared, but because I can't wait to see what else she's done. I sprint through the kitchen and as I thought, my hunch was right. The dirty doors of the greenhouse are now crystal clear and the vines that divide the glass are alive and green. I open the doors and as impossible as it may be, the greenhouse is even more beautiful than the gardens outside. Strange, lush plants grow from every planter, so full that their leaves and flowers curl over and fill the aisles. It's like a colorful jungle and the air is full of scents, more amazing than any perfume I've ever smelled. I step carefully down into the greenhouse, so that I don't hurt even one leaf of these amazing plants. Slowly, I make my way through the thick leaves and vines and pop out just beyond the huge tree. In front of me, "The Nana" is standing beside the wall of cabinets.

"You did all this?" I ask, even though I already know the answer and although she can read my mind, she nods and says softly:

"A little help from the earth,

and seeds by the pound.

All I did was make beauty,

grow out of the ground."

"The Nana" bangs her cane on the ground and suddenly the heavy book that the Shadow stole, appears and hovers between her and I.

"The book! You wrote it?" I ask and the book floats over to me. I put my arms out and it lands softly in them as "The Nana" continues:

"The book wrote itself.

It's meant only for your eye.

So even I cannot decipher it,

or the most evil that'll try.

Last night I took a journey,

and chased a Shadow down a hole,

to get back something precious,

that from my grandson, it stole.

This is your own book of spells,

you're one of our kind.

But, you must start the first lesson,

you're falling behind."

With everything that's happened, I hadn't given much thought to the fact that I'm related to her.

"Our kind? You mean I'm magic too?" My voice cracks a little and she replies:

"Much more than just magic,

a warrior you are,

like all those that came before you,

since the first twinkling star.

Our last name, Kokotilo,

is given to those who will fight.

The evils of childhood,

the things that go bump in the night."

"Hang on." I say. "You want me to fight those Shadows? I'm terrified of them!"

"The Nana" crosses her legs, floats over to me:

"We thought we had defeated them,

a long time ago,

but the things that have been scaring you,

prove that isn't so.

You are only scared,

of what you don't understand.

You are a warrior Calium,

which gives you the upper hand."

"Wow." I say with a smile. "I'm a warrior? Cool. I guess if you teach me the magic and stuff I can try and fight those monsters."

"The Nana" tilts her head:

"I will teach you all that I know,

but your courage you've already found.

Without magic you've already defeated,

those Shadows on the playground.

Now start with the lesson,

in the book of old,

and the rest of the answers,

will begin to unfold."

"The Nana" raises her hand and Tommy, my tomato plant, appears on top of the stone table. She then gives me a wink and floats off towards the kitchen. It's now or never. She says I'm a warrior…that's the best news I've heard in a while! If my Grandma, who can bend walls back and fly, thinks I can do this, than so do I.

So, I walk over to the table and open the heavy bark cover, but once again all I see are symbols.

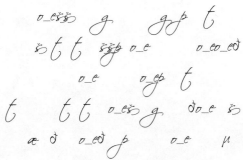

How am I supposed to start my lesson if I can't read the book? As I stare at the symbols, I remember something "The

Nana" said. This book is just for me. No one else can understand it. It can only be read by my eye…my eye…she didn't say eyes. That's it! I close my left eye and suddenly the symbols change to words.

Lesson 1: Growing potion.
For this spell you will need:
One wobble pot,
Two bottles of golden soil
And one drop of blue-bloom

I open up the cabinets to look for the supplies I need. In the bottom cabinet I find some oddly shaped pots, so I pull one out. The bottom of the pot is round, not flat and as I set it down on the table it starts to wobble back and forth on its rounded bottom.

"Wobble Pot? Check! This is easy."

I open the next cabinet, but don't see anything that looks like golden soil, so I move on to the one above it. This cabinet is filled with bottles of yellow colored dirt, but there are like five rows of bottles and each row is a different shade of yellow. How do I know which one is gold? Think Cailum, think…yes, that's it. I carefully run through the leaves and go into the kitchen. "The Nana" is sitting by the fireplace drinking tea.

"Hey Nana, no time to talk, learning," I say and open the junk drawer.

I grab a battery, a flashlight and run carefully back to the stone table. I take apart the flashlight, so that all I'm left with is the bulb, two wires. I then pull out one bottle of each shade of dirt and make five tiny piles. I hold one of the wires that are attached to the bulb, against the bottom of the battery with my finger. Then, one by one, I put the top of the battery against each pile and touch the other wire to the other side. I do this to the first four piles and nothing happens. Then finally, as I put the battery top against the last pile and touch the other wire to the side, the light bulb lights up! I learned in science class that gold was the best conductor of electricity, so this pile must be gold!! I take two bottles of the soil out of the cabinet and place it beside the pot. Now, for the last ingredient, the "Blue-Bloom." I open the top cabinet and once again I'm confused. Inside there are many vials of liquid, but all the liquids are clear. Each of them has a label, but of course none of them are labeled Blue-Bloom. This is not as easy as I thought. I start to sort through the vials and place each one of them on the table. Anger, Happiness, Joy, Excitement…what kind of names of plant foods are these? I figure that I must have the wrong cabinet, so I search through all the others, but none of them have anything in them labeled Blue-Bloom. I look back at the vials lined up on the table. Anger, Happiness, Joy, Excitement…what do they have in common? Well, they're all feelings. Okay, so what's blue?…

blue...If I'm feeling blue…I'm feeling sad! I jump up and start rooting through the cabinet again. At the very back, where I can barely reach, is a vial named Sadness! I stand on my tippy toes, pull it out and set it beside the rest of the supplies. Time to turn the page in the old book and read on.

Step 1:

Place a plant that you know, like the back of your hand, that has been grown by hand, into the wobble pot

"Well, I've been reseeding Tommy for four years now, so I think he'll do."

I gently pull him out of the pot he's in, shake the old dirt off and place him in the wobble pot. Move'n on to step two.

Step 2:

Cover the plants roots with golden soil.

"Simple enough." I say and open the cork tops on two bottles of the golden soil.

I carefully sprinkle them into the pot so that they cover Tommy's roots. I then grab the vial of Blue-Bloom and squeeze the top of the eyedropper, sucking liquid up into it. I hold it over the golden soil and squeeze the rubber top. Two drops of liquid fall out of the dropper, turn blue and then disappear into the shiny golden soil. Instantly I hear a rumble and the wobble pot starts to shake. It rolls back and forth on its round base, so

I step back. The pot begins to bounce up and down violently, banging on the stone table until a puff of blue smoke rises from the pot and then everything stops. The thick smoke smells like an old gym sock and I start to cough. I wave my hands back and forth, trying to clear the air and as I do, I see that Tommy is gone! What? This was supposed to be growth potion, not "vaporize your plant potion". I cautiously move towards the pot, like walking up to a dud firecracker that hasn't exploded. About a foot away, I stretch my arm out, lean my head back and try to touch the pot…BANG! A thick vine shoots up from the golden soil and into the air, so high it smashes through a pane of glass in the roof. I cover my head as pieces of glass fall down around me. What was once my tiny little tomato plant is now taller than the big tree in the middle and towers over me. Floppy leaves as wide as Old Rusty and bright red tomatoes as big as my head sprout out all over Tommy's huge stalk.

"Holy Jack and the Bean Stalk! What did I do wrong?"

I hear a thud and look back at the stone table. The book is flapping it's heavy covers, up and down, banging them against the table, as if it's trying to get my attention. I step back to the book, lean over it and as I do, it turns it's own page over.

Step 4:

Never skip a step.

"Perfect! My first magic potion and I totally pwned

myself." Reluctantly, I read on.

Step 5:

If you skip step 4, clean up the broken glass.

"Ha, ha, ha. Very funny."

Great, not only does this book have a sick sense of humor, but it's also right. I can't leave broken glass all over the floor, Aidan could walk in here at anytime and the feet on his pajamas won't protect him from sharp pieces of glass. But there's no way I'm gonna find a broom in here now that it's filled with all these thick plants, so I'm gonna have to improvise. I look around and spy a big empty pot and tip it over and then use my slipper to brush the broken glass into it. Perfect, now back to my lesson.

Step 6:

Use one drop of Blue-Bloom for growth, two drops to climb.

Got it. One drop for growth, two drops to climb. No more mistakes. Now I need to find another plant. I reach down to put my slipper back on and...

"uh, oh!" I accidentally knock the vial of Blue-Bloom all over my arm. "This can't be good."

What should I do? What should I do? I know...the book. It'll have the answer. I turn the page, hoping the book has some sort of "What to do if" section at the end of the lesson. Great, found it. I take a deep breath and read it carefully.

What to do if:

HANG ON!!!!!!!

"What?"

Suddenly, my arm starts to twitch out of control and bangs against the table just like the wobble pot did. I grab my arm with my other hand and try to hold it still, but it's no use. BANG! A puff of blue smoke fills the air, covering my arm and I hold my breath. I'm not holding it because of the smell this time, I'm holding it hoping that my arm hasn't disappeared! When I can't hold my breath any longer, I blow the cloud of smoke away and...my arm is still there! Whew, I guess the potion only works on plants, not people. I look at my arm closely, making sure it's okay and it is, that is, until the sun hits it. As the bright sunlight shines through Tommy's leaves, my skin starts moving back and forth on its own, like snakeskin crackling and twisting. I feel sick to my stomach, my head aches and my eyes begin to blur. I blink them a couple of times, trying not to faint, but it's no use. I'm going down. THUD!

I'm not sure how long I've been out for, but as I open my eyes, I realize my stomach no longer feels sick. I reach up to pull myself off the floor and as I grab the edge of the stone table, something feels odd. The table doesn't feel like cold stone, it feels like warm wood. I look up to see what happened to the table and almost pass out again. It's not the table that's changed, it's my arm! From my elbow down, thick wooden bark grows towards my hand and where it reaches the place my fingers used to be it, changes into green vines! I let go of the table with my vine fingers and shake my arm, but it won't come off!

"AAAAAAHHHHHHHHH!!!!!!!" I hear a scream, but it's not me, it's Aidan. I turn around expecting to see him behind me, terrified of my mutant hand, but he's not there.

"AAAAAAAHHHHHHHH!!!!!" I hear him again and it's coming from the kitchen.

Whatever's making him freak out, it isn't me, but it must be bad, because he only screams like that when he's terrified or in trouble or both. I start running towards the greenhouse doors, suddenly more worried about him than my arm. In front of me, the thick leaves and vines that hang over the aisle lift up and move out of the way, making a clear path for me. I burst through the doors, ready to fight and "The Nana" raises her hand, motioning for me to stop. Aidan stands in the middle of the kitchen, holding a chip clip in each of his mittens. He swings the clips like weapons at "The Nana" and yells.

"Sashawn, Pashawn, PEA!!!"

This must be one of her lessons so I wait and watch as she moves towards him, speaking softly:

"I don't understand this language you speak,

is it something you made it up in your head?

You must use real words my little Aidan,

it makes no sense, all these words that you've said."

Aidan lowers his chip clips in frustration and then points them at the pantry.

"Pashawn!"

The pantry doors burst open and cans of food fly everywhere. Aidan raises his clips up and a huge Shadow jumps out, tackling him to the ground. Aidan rolls across the floor, wrapped up in the Shadow, trying to fight it off.

"PASHAWN, SASHAWN." He screams and I yell at "The Nana" "Do something!" but she doesn't move.

Angry and frustrated I tell her again, "Help him? You're the one with magic powers?" but still she just stands there.

This might be some sort of practice to her, but that Shadow might really hurt Aidan.

"Fine. If you won't help him, I will!" I snap, and jump towards them wrestling on the ground.

"The Nana" slams her cane on the ground, sending a blast of blue light shooting towards me, freezing me in mid-air. Unable to move, all I can do now is watch as the Shadow holds Aidan down and he screams for my help. The Shadow begins dragging Aidan across the floor towards the pantry and finally "The Nana" moves. As she steps towards the Shadow, it stops and rises up, like a bear on it's back legs, ready to attack. "The Nana" points her cane towards the Shadow and it changes from it's Shadow form into a brown, scruffy, half dog, half pig monster, with long bottom teeth that poke out over it's top lip, like a wart hog. The beast bares it's teeth at "The Nana", snorts and then drops back down, pinning Aidan to the floor. It growls, as it opens it's slobbery mouth over Aidan's face and moves in to bite him.

"YIELD!!!!"

"The Nana's" voice shakes the room like thunder and the beast stops and glares at her. She continues to speak in a strong, masterful voice:

> *"It's a Frust-Ration Aidan,*
> *made of your parents' divorce.*
> *It gains strength from your anger,*
> *your hurting is the source.*
> *You have the power, young warrior,*
> *to defeat it with your voice,*
> *but only REAL words will affect it,*
> *YOU DO NOT HAVE A CHOICE!"*

The Frust-Ration shakes it's head and again opens it's jaws, pushing it's snarled teeth towards Aidan's face. Aidan's arms shake as he tries to hold it back, but the monster is too strong and as it forces it's head down, Aidan's elbows begin to bend.

I beg "The Nana", "Please help him! He can't hold that thing back for much longer!"

She looks at me and then slams her cane down on the ground and says in a loud, thunderous voice:

"MAKE YOURSELF HEARD,

USE YOUR WORDS!!!!!!!"

Aidan clinches his lips tight together. His face goes red, like you're holding your breath and from deep down inside him, he begins to make a strange sound. It starts like a whimper, then changes into a deep long groan. The terrified look on his face turns into anger and he opens his mouth, letting out a sound.

"L..."

As the sound shoots out of his mouth it becomes a shiny silver letter that spins through the air and hits the Frust-Ration like a punch. The monster winces as the letter cuts into it's cheek and stays embedded, like a throwing star. Aidan continues to make the sounds...

"E"... "T"

The two letters hit the beast hard, knocking it's head back and Aidan, seeing it's working, groans again, to summon more words.

"M...E...G...O!"

The letters shoot out of Aidan's mouth and hit the beast

in the chest, knocking it off of him. The Frust-Ration is sent flying across the room and crashes through a stack of plates on the table. Aidan jumps to his feet, covering his mouth and looks at me startled. I can tell by the look in his eyes that this new power frightens him. As he looks to me for help, the Frust-Ration sees the gap in Aidan's attack and pounces towards him then disappears in mid-air. "The Nana" calls Aidan's attention back to the fight:

> *"This monster was created,*
>
> *by the feelings you've kept inside.*
>
> *Leave no feeling unsaid,*
>
> *give the beast nowhere to hide.*
>
> *Loose your frustration,*
>
> *say what is true.*
>
> *Let out the feelings,*
>
> *that have been silencing you!"*

Aidan nods to "The Nana", uncovers his mouth, shouts into the air.

"W...h...y...c...ouldn't you guy's work it out? You didn't eever try!"

Instantly, the Frust-Ration appears and the words hit the beast like machine gun bullets, knocking it out of the air and onto the floor. Aidan keeps shouting, not giving the monster another chance to recover.

"You were wrong! Everything is not okay. I'm not okay. This divorce isn't fair!"

Instead of anger this time, his face looks sad and as the letters leave his mouth, he begins to cry. He covers his little face with his mittens and runs over to "The Nana", who wraps him in her arms:

"There, there little warrior,

it will all be alright.

You gave your feelings words,

and filled your dark space with light."

Hearing my little brother's pain put into words sends tears running down my cheeks. As I watch her gently rock him from side to side, out of the corner of my eye, I see something move. Behind them, by the cupboards, the Frust-Ration stumbles to it's feet and I scream, "Watch out!"

"The Nana" turns around, claps her hands and I fall out of the air, landing in front of the monster. No longer frozen, I point my wooden arm towards the snarling beast and shout "Leave my brother alone!"

Suddenly, vines shoot out of the fingers of my bark covered arm, wrap around the beast and I slam it into the counter. A cloud of white fills the air as bag of flour gets crushed between the beast and the counter top. "The Nana" tells Aidan:

"Let's finish this,

call it by name.

The words will send this Frust-Ration,

back to the Emaji-Nation, from whence it came."

"The Nana" slams her cane against the ground and a swirling portal of light appears, bending back the floorboards below her. Aidan lets go of her and looks the beast straight in the eyes. I move the struggling beast in front of the portal and Aidan shouts, "Take your FRUSTRATION back!"

My vines release as the words slam into the Frust-Ration, knocking it down into the portal. "The Nana" then slams her cane on the ground and the swirling portal closes.

"Are you okay?" I say to Aidan.

"I'm great." He replies with a huge grin.

"You don't know how happy I am to hear you say that…" I smile, "Well, actually to hear you say anything at all."

"The Nana" clears her throat, straightens her robe and says softly:

"You must not tell your mother,

about this Shadow fight.

She is not ready to accept that you are warriors,

but I will tell her when the time is right.

You both are far more powerful,

than before I've ever seen,

and you've proved in just the first lesson,

you know how to work as a team.

But before we move forward,

your warrior names you will hear.

Names given by your ancient ancestors,

names the Emaji-Nation will come to fear."

She raises her cane above my head. It starts to glow and then she lowers it slowly onto my shoulder, like a king does to a knight:

"Warrior of things that grow,

flower, plant and tree.

You will be known for evermore,

as Vita-Man C."

She lifts the cane off my shoulder, then lowers it onto Aidan's:

"You are silent, quick and strong,

in all of your ways.

You will be known as The Mitt Ninja,

for the rest of your days."

"The Nana" raises the cane off of his shoulder, holds it above her head and spins it in the air. Waves of blue light, like the ones in the hall, fall like a waterfall and surround Aidan and I.

"What's happening?" Aidan asks me.

"I don't know." I answer and as I do Aidan begins to change.

His saggy Dalmatian pajamas change into a black ninja

outfit, filled with muscles. The hood becomes a mask, covering his head and face and the black spots turn to white. Across his chest is a belt of golden chip clips, his mittens sparkle with blue light and his ninja shoes are tied up by ruby red straps. Everything about him is different, except for his eyes and the puppy ears on the top of his hood.

"Aidan…you look like a super hero!" I say and his eyes open wide.

"I do? Look at you!"

I turn and catch my reflection in the greenhouse doors and jump back, because it looks nothing like me. There is now a black mask, like a raccoon around my eyes and green warrior paint on my cheeks. My hair stands straight up in a Mohawk and a cape of leaves hangs from my neck. There are silver shields over my knees and a belt with a golden Trowel hanging around my waist. Green vines move up and down my right arm and my cape flaps behind me, even though there is no wind. "The Nana" floats above us, looking proud:

> *"We may have won that battle,*
> *but we have yet to win the war.*
> *The Emaji-Nation was just testing you,*
> *I'm sure there's more evil they have in store.*
> *With the appearance of that messenger,*
> *they have begun their attack.*

We must continue your training immediately,

so you are ready when they come back."

"The Nana" slams her cane against the ground and in the reflection of the doors I see we've been instantly changed back into our normal selves.

"What is going on in here?" I hear Mama say.

As "The Nana" steps aside and I see Mama standing in the kitchen doorway with her arms crossed.

"Did a bomb go off in here?" she says, looking around the kitchen covered in flour and broken stuff from the fight. "You boys are in a heap of trouble..." she starts to say, but before she can say another word, "The Nana" jumps in:

"I was trying to make pancakes,

I must be getting old.

It's not the boys' fault, Nini,

they only did what they were told."

Mama looks at "The Nana" suspiciously.

"Pancakes? You mean to tell me that this disaster zone was caused by pancakes?"

She starts picking up pieces of broken plates and cans and by the look on her face, it's clear she isn't buying it. "Ma you promised..."

She glares at "The Nana" and Aidan steps in front of her.

"Please don't be mad Mama." he says and everything in

219

Mama's arms crashes on the floor.

Her face suddenly goes white and she looks like she is gonna faint.

"What did you say?" she asks hesitantly.

Aidan looks at her with his big, puppy dog eyes and replies, "I said, don't be mad."

Mama falls to her knees and burst into tears.

"Oh, my baby. You're talking…I…I…" Aidan hugs her and says "It's okay Mama. "The Nana" helped me speak." Mama squeezes Aidan so tight, I think his head is gonna pop off.

"Thank you Ma. Thank you for giving me my little boy back." she says over Aidan's shoulder.

"We're sorry about the mess Mama. I'll clean it up." I tell her and she reaches out and pulls me into her arms.

"Who cares about the mess?" she says laughing, "He's speaking again! Let the Shadows clean it up! We're going out for breakfast!"

We went for breakfast to a little diner in town that Mama said she used to come to when she was a teenager. It reminds me of the greasy spoon Aidan and I used to wait at while Mama and Dad were in counselling, only there are no awkward silences at this place. Mama was so happy to have Aidan speaking again, that she told us we could order anything we wanted. I got "The

Lumberjack's Breakfast" with "Extra logs" and Aidan got the "Eiffel Tower", a stack of French toast that I swear was taller than he was. I guess fighting monsters makes you build up a "Monster" of an appetite. As we stuffed our faces, I noticed that "The Nana" only ordered tea, black with no sugar. I offered her some of my "lumberjack" but she said:

"I only eat things,

that will wither and fade,

These things you eat here,

are full of chemicals and man made."

Well, she is probably right, but mmmmmm, it sure tastes good. There was a lot of laughter at our table and talking, well mostly Aidan talking, but that was all right, cause he had a lot to say and we wanted to hear it. I know that Aidan and I wanted to talk about the battle, but "The Nana" told us Mama wasn't ready to accept that we were warriors. So, we carried on, like a normal family just eating breakfast at a diner, not like a couple of warriors that had just kicked serious scruffy, monster butt in their kitchen. But, every once in a while, when Mama wasn't looking, "The Nana" would smile and wink at us and we would wink back.

Old Rusty was running better than ever, she didn't sputter or belch smoke as we drove through downtown Peterborough on our way back to Kokotilo Manor. It wasn't just our car and the

Manor, even this old town seemed to have gotten better overnight. The streets are filled with bright sunlight and the planters that line the sidewalks are now filled with the same colorful flowers as our garden. I'm not the only one that's noticed the change in this dark dreary town; the streets are filled with smiling people, all staring in awe at the flowers that have seemed to appear overnight. Mama turns to "The Nana" and whispered so that we won't hear, "Ma, what have you done?"

"The Nana" rolls down her window and says as she smells the sweet air:

"Our family built this town,

it is our responsibility to look after.

You're not the only one,

who needed the help of a Mast-Her."

Standing outside the Ice Cream Shop, I see Rachel, so I shout out the window to her, "Hey, Rachel!"

She sees and points at the flowers, yelling back, "Who did this?"

I want to tell her so bad about my Nana, about her magic and our battle with the Frust-Ration, but all I can do is shrug my shoulders as we drive by.

We pull up to the Manor and suddenly I remember the colossal mess we left in the kitchen. Aidan and I drag ourselves into the kitchen, knowing there's at least a couple of hours of work waiting for us. I walk into the kitchen and open the pantry to grab the broom.

Aidan shouts "Look!"

I jump and swing the broom around, expecting to see a Shadow ready to attack, but there is no Shadow. There is no monster, no Shadow and NO MESS!

"Having a Nana Rocks!" Aidan says.

I laugh "Do you think she will do our homework too?"

"The Nana" appears in front of us:

> *I would never do anything dishonest,*
>
> *for when you do you will get caught,*
>
> *so in answer to your question,*
>
> *absolutely, positively, unequivocally not."*

"How are you boys making out in there?" Mama asks.

"Just finishing up." I say as she walks in.

"Wow!" she gasps, "You boys are fast! Now if I could only get you to help me tidy up the rest of the house."

"The Nana" smiles and nods:

> *"The boys were just saying,*
>
> *they wanted to help you more,*
>
> *so I made a list for each of them,*
>
> *of all the Manor's chores."*

"The Nana" winks at us and pulls two pieces of paper out from behind her back. She hands them to Aidan and I.

"What's this?" Aidan asks.

"A list of chores." I grumble back. What? I thought that we needed to start our training. Come on! This is pure agony, like when your parents make you pause a video game right at the best part. Aidan looks mad too.

"Chores?" he scoffs at "The Nana" and she replies:

"If you take care of this home,

it will take care of you.

Chores are just part of what,

all families must do.

There is much to be learned,

it doesn't take long.

Contributing to your home,

can make you wise and strong.

By hand this house was built,

and by hand it will stand.

You must nurture and protect it,

one day this will all be your land."

"Great!" Mama says with a huge smile on her face, "Lets get started."

Now, normally I'd whine and mope until Mama just got frustrated enough to do it herself. But maybe this is part of the training. Maybe it will make us stronger. After all, she is the one with the magic cane, so I think we'd better go along with it.

For the rest of the day we cleaned, scrubbed, polished and cut. It wasn't all that bad. I actually felt good, seeing the difference we made to the house and as strange as it sounds, it made the house feel more like my own. I kept waiting for a moment, to talk with "The Nana" about our powers, about everything. I have so many questions, but Mama stayed glued to us. As bummed as I am, after avoiding Mama for like a week, building the fort, I guess we owe her at least one day together.

Right after dinner Aidan and I went up to bed. Mama wanted to snuggle in and watch a movie, but honestly I was pooped and Aidan kept nodding off at the dinner table. She'd already seen the fort, so there was no need to hide it from her and Aidan and I let Mama tuck us in. As she walked out of our room, she pointed to the words we wrote on the cardboard roof.

"By the way. Mama's roof? That's not a Mama's roof. That my boys, is a cardboard-Mama not included, epic fail! Next time you build a fort, leave the roof to me."

It's been about a half an hour since she turned off the light and closed our door. Now, with "The Nana" just down the hall, I don't need to put the locks on the door or turn on all the flashlights, I can just lay here, staring into the darkness. What a day. What a long, long day. My eyes begin to feel heavy and I let them close, without fear.

Something's on my chest, I can't open my eyes. I can't breathe.

"Expecting an Old Hag?" a dark, sinister voice growls, sending shivers up my spine.

My eyes open and I want to scream…but I can't.

"Never send a women to do a man's job." I hear it laugh.

I look down and there's a boot pressing into my chest. It's black and has insects crawling all over it! My eyes follow the boot up to the bottom of a purple robe. It's tattered and torn full of holes. My eyes follow the dirty, white fur that runs along the edges and stop on a huge, grey hand. The nails are yellow, like the monster in Dad's closet. But on every finger of this huge hand there are rings made of living bugs.

"UP HERE!" The voice grumbles.

I look up and all I can see in the darkness are yellow glowing eyes.

"BOOOO!" It shouts and if I could jump I would.

It moves it's face into the moonlight and I wish now it were the Old Hag. It's a man, an old, angry man. His yellow eyes are the only color on his grey, wrinkly, face and his has a long pointy nose that hangs over his mouth, that's full of cracked, dirty teeth. He has a matted, brown beard, full of bugs and long hair that's all tied in knots. On top of his head, he's wearing a dented, twisted crown, lined with jewels. He leans down and puts his face so close to me, I can smell his breath, and it smells like a dead rat.

"Oh that poor old shriveled grape. Still sending children to fight me. So you're next, huh. Do you think <u>you</u> can defeat me? Of course you can't. I could crush you right here, right now."

He presses down harder with the boot on my chest and suddenly, I cant breathe at all.

"You're not a warrior, you're a kid. A little, kid who made his Daddy go away. You can't even get your parents back together because you're not good enough. So how do you think you're going to defeat me?"

I start to see spots, like when I fainted during the Christmas concert and I know I'm about to black out. My ears start to ring, louder and louder. Everything's going dark. He's laughing, but as the ringing in my ears begins to drown out his horrible voice. I'm disappearing into the darkness. I'm fading. Fading away from my room, my Mama, my.... I hear someone yelling.

"NAAANAAAA!"...It's Aidan. I waited so long to hear his voice, and now I think it's the last voice I'll ever hear...